Patches of Light

Short Stories from the Cheshire Prize for Literature 2015

Edited by Ian Seed

University of Chester Press

First published 2016
by University of Chester Press
Parkgate Road
Chester CH1 4BJ

Printed and bound in the UK by the
LIS Print Unit
University of Chester
Cover designed by the LIS Graphics Team
University of Chester

Editorial Material
© University of Chester, 2016
Foreword, Stories and Poems
© the respective authors, 2016

All Rights Reserved
No part of this publication may be reproduced, stored in a retrieval system or transmitted in any form or by any means without the prior permission of the copyright owner, other than as permitted by UK copyright legislation or under the terms and conditions of a recognised copyright licensing scheme

A catalogue record of this book is available
from the British Library

ISBN 978-1-908258-29-8

CONTENTS

Contributors	viii
Foreword	xv
Tick Tock *Pauline Brown*	1
Purdy *Andrew Fleming*	7
The Time Traveller's Daughter *Jan Kaneen*	14
Water World *Sue Hoffmann*	20
The Swimming Pool *Liz Milne*	27
Honey for the Bag Lady *Valentine Williams*	34
The Harvester *Laura Thompson*	40
My Will Ne'er Be Done *Lynne Parry-Griffiths*	43

Patches of Light

Cursed *Gordon Williams*	51
Envelopes *Heather Freckleton*	57
Hallqueen *Roy Gray*	62
Weeding *Robert Angus*	68
I'd Like to Settle Down But They Won't Let Me *Ian Pickering*	73
Making Amends to a Fallen Angel *Lynne Voyce*	79
Darren Whittaker *Barbara Oldham*	86
Lost in Transit *Dominic Teague*	92
Pig Man *Margaret Holbrook*	99
A Civilised Marriage *Tom Kilcourse*	103

Contents

The Writing Game   109
David Bryan

For Yourself Alone   116
Cathy Bryant

Female 198   122
Annest Gwilym

CONTRIBUTORS

Robert Angus is a retired radiologist who after a lifetime of writing factual scientific reports is trying to learn how to write fiction. When he isn't reading or writing or doing his share of the cooking and housework, he likes to tear around Cheshire and North Wales on his motorbike with all the other grey haired motorcyclists.

Pauline Brown grew up and went to school in Macclesfield. She has a degree in English and Drama, and after moving to London she worked for many years in film production. Since enrolling on a creative writing course three years ago, her achievements have included twice winning Flash500, an honorary mention in the Fish Short Story Prize, and being shortlisted for the Bridport Prize for flash fiction. She feels thrilled and honoured to have been awarded first place in the Cheshire Prize for Literature.

David Bryan started writing comedy 25 years ago to earn a few quid while looking after his young son at home. Besides selling articles, fillers and jokes to various magazines, he also had sketches on British and German TV. On returning to conventional employment, he tried his hand at poetry and has had more than 100 poems published in various magazines. Recently, he has been working on short stories and flash fiction.

Cathy Bryant worked as a life model, civil servant and child minder before becoming a professional writer. She has won twenty-two literary awards, including the Bulwer-Lytton Fiction Prize and the Wergle Flomp Humor Poetry Contest, and her work has appeared in more than 200 publications. Cathy's books are: *Contains Strong Language and Scenes of a Sexual Nature* and *Look at All the Women* (poetry), *How to Win Writing Competitions* (non-fiction) and *Pride & Regicide – a Mary Bennet Mystery* (novel). See her online listings for cash-strapped writers at Cathy's Comps & Calls, updated on the first of every month. Cathy lives in Cheshire, UK.

Andrew Fleming works in higher education and lives in Lancashire with his wife, daughter and rescue whippet. His writing has appeared in a number of anthologies, magazines and journals and has been broadcast on BBC Radio Merseyside. He is currently working on his first novel.

Heather Freckleton has lived in numerous locations in the UK and spent a short time in India. She has now settled in Hull, soon to be City of Culture. She feels amazingly fortunate to have won prizes for her short stories and poetry and to have appeared in various anthologies. She feels compelled to write even though this can feel like swimming through treacle wearing a heavy back pack! She spends her time dreaming and gazing over the Humber and just fitting the rest in.

Roy Gray lives in Macclesfield and has authored a few published short stories and non-fiction. These have been published in *Interzone Magazine*, *Sci Phi Journal*, *Physics World*, *Packaging India*, etc. Some of his 'poems' are available online. He is not the Roy Gray who writes erotic poetry, which you may also find online. His chapbook *The Joy of Technology* was published by Pendragon Press in 2011 and is now a self-published e-book, which might persuade some he is that other, but there are at least two Roy Grays and this Roy's poetic efforts remain decidedly chaste.

Annest Gwilym lives in North Wales, near the Snowdonia National Park, with her Jack Russell terrier. Her writing has been published in a number of literary magazines including *Ariadne's Thread*, *The Cannon's Mouth*, *The Journal*, *Clear Poetry* and on *writersbillboard.net*. A couple of her poems were published in the Templar anthology *Mill* in November 2015. She has received four 'Special Commendations' and one 'Shortlisted' in writing competitions in recent years.

Sue Hoffmann is a retired teacher from Wirral. She has an MA in Language Teaching and Learning. Sixteen of her short stories have been published in anthologies, newspapers, magazines or online and

Contributors

she has won four writing competitions. She enjoys visiting local primary and secondary schools to lead creative writing workshops based on her 'crossover' fantasy novel, *High King*, which was published in 2013 by Circaidy Gregory Press.

Margaret Holbrook still lives in Cheshire, where she grew up. She writes poetry, plays and fiction. In 2014, her short story 'Our Brian' was longlisted for the BBC Radio 4 programme, *Opening Lines*. Several of her short stories have been published in magazines and anthologies.

Jan Kaneen is a graduate in English Literature from University College of Wales Aberystwyth but only because, back in 1983, Creative Writing was not an option. When she took early retirement from Muir Housing (based in Chester) in 2014, she signed up for a Creative Writing module with the Open University. Once she started writing stories she found she couldn't stop. She now lives in a hobbit hole in flattest Cambridgeshire Fenland concocting weird and not-so-weird short stories and flash fiction, channelling voices who have tales they must tell.

Tom Kilcourse retired in the 1990s and went to live in Normandy with his wife. They returned to England in 2013 and settled in Cuddington, Northwich with their dog, Frenchie. Tom is a compulsive writer who, in addition to his fiction, writes a monthly essay for an online publisher. He wrote his first short stories in 1977 and has published two collections, both of which are on Amazon along with his novels.

Liz Milne has three children, two cats and one husband. Born and raised in Zimbabwe, she moved to Chester in 2004, having learned to love the city while visiting as a child – it felt like coming home … She is currently studying Creative Writing and English Literature at the University of Chester and hopes to be able to write full time one day.

Barbara Oldham is growing old disgracefully whilst wearing purple. She enjoys theatre-going, languages and visiting new places. Under pressure she confesses to being something of a stationery-aholic with a vast pencil collection.

Lynne Parry-Griffiths lives and teaches in North Wales. She has an MA in Creative Writing and her story 'Window Dressing' was included in a previous Cheshire Prize Anthology. She is currently taking time out from writing historical fiction and is working on her first Young Adult novel.

Ian Pickering has lived in Northwich all his life and works for a large engineering company in Knutsford. He has an understanding wife called Mandy, three understanding children called Sam, Beth and Maddie and a totally baffled dog called Daisy. He

Contributors

believes in writing about what you know. Hence his story in this volume is set in a pub. Ian's only previous claim to fame is reaching the final of television's *Mastermind* in 2003. Hopefully this will give him something else to talk about.

Dominic Teague was born in Chester and presently resides there. He studied English Language and Literature at the University of Liverpool and has written scripts for several British comic books, including *2000 AD* and *Commando*.

Laura Thompson has lived in Stockport all her life. She is currently a finalist (final year student) reading English at the University of Cambridge, where outside of her studies she runs the college Literary Society and allotments.

Lynne Voyce has had almost fifty short stories published and been placed in many competitions. Her first short story collection, *Kirigami*, was published by Ink Tears Press in December 2014. While continuing to write short fiction, she is currently working on her first novel. Having grown up in Ellesmere Port, she now lives in Birmingham with her husband and two daughters, where she teaches in an inner city comprehensive school. This is Lynne's third appearance in a Cheshire Prize anthology.

Gordon Williams was born in Prestbury and has lived in Northern Ireland since 1984. He has an MA in Creative Writing and has won fourteen prizes in story competitions. He's had short stories published in magazines and anthologies and on several websites and is slowly revising his first novel.

Valentine Williams (Mary) lurks in a Shropshire cottage with a well under the floor and writes dark fiction. After gaining an MA at Edge Hill, she was commissioned to write two self-help books and has since published four novels, poetry and a collection of short stories, *Unconfirmed Reports From Out There*. Her latest novel *Losing It*, is published by Tirgearr Press. She has a background in teaching and psychotherapy, and has four sons but no cat as yet. She has won awards for poetry and stories.

Ian Seed (editor) is Lecturer in Creative Writing, and Programme Leader for the BA in Creative Writing, at the University of Chester. His poetry, short stories, articles and translations have appeared in numerous journals and anthologies. He is the author of a number of collections of poetry and short-short fiction. His latest book, *Identity Papers*, was published by Shearsman in February 2016 and featured on BBC Radio 3's *The Verb* in March.

FOREWORD

'The great thing about a short story,' said Emma Donoghue, 'is that it doesn't have to trawl through someone's whole life; it can come in glancingly from the side.' Each story in this anthology does precisely that – enters a life 'glancingly' but illuminates what is truly important about that life in the process of doing so. Avoiding glib, ready-made solutions, the best short stories, like poems, offer an authentic navigation of the complex situations we often find ourselves in. The world we inhabit is fast-changing, never quite the same from one moment to the next. It has perhaps been ever thus. The ancient Greek philosopher Heraclitus famously said that we never step into the same river twice. Yet with so much to distract and entice us today, how can we know what is 'real', what has any kind of genuine worth? Does it really matter?

The stories here do not pretend to know the answers. Rather they seek to reflect and explore the hopes, dreams, joys, fears and frailties that are common to us all, but which are revealed differently in each life. They may offer us only glimpses, but each glimpse will leave us changed in some way. Like shifting patches of light on water, they invite us to stop and look, to linger for a brief space of time, to take away something we felt we always knew, but didn't know that we knew before.

Patches of Light

Each story in *Patches of Light* creates, occupies and draws us into its own particular universe, but all the stories talk to one another in the themes they explore, such as childhood, youth, age, memory, love, loss, betrayal, and trying to be good. This collection travels from the tragic to the comic, the real to the surreal, and the dramatic to the meditative, sometimes all within one story. It does its job of opening our eyes, getting under our skin, and making us listen.

The challenge for this year's Cheshire Prize for Literature Competition has been especially tough for the entrants: to write a short story in just 1,500 words. This is by no means an easy thing to do (if you don't believe me try it for yourself). As Truman Capote pointed out, the short story is 'the most difficult and disciplining form of prose writing extant'. How does one, for example, write about child abuse within such limitations without coming across as sensationalist, or exploitative, or – heaven forbid – sentimental? Yet Pauline Brown in her story 'Tick Tock' is able to navigate this extraordinarily difficult subject through use of ellipsis, understatement, sensory detail and an astonishingly subtle use of a child's point of view. After some discussion, the Panel of Judges agreed unanimously that 'Tick Tock' should be awarded First Prize. It was selected from a total of 226 entries. The three runners up also offer original, striking and compelling examples of the

Foreword

short story form. They are (in alphabetical order by surname): 'For Yourself Alone' by Cathy Bryant, 'Female 198' by Annest Gwilym and 'My Will Ne'er Be Done' by Lynne-Parry Griffiths. The other short stories selected for this anthology do what the best fiction should: entertain, discomfort, and reveal the truth in unexpected places through their shifting patches of dark and light.

I would like to offer my deepest thanks to my fellow judges: Carys Davies, prize-winning author of a number of short-story collections, and John Scrivener, long-standing judge of the Cheshire Prize for Literature. Their invaluable help in the judging process and in making the final selections for the prizes, as well as in making suggestions for the anthology, has made all the difference. This anthology would not be here without them. I am grateful to the High Sheriff of Cheshire, Bill Holroyd, for announcing the winners' names, presenting them with their prizes, and helping to make the awards evening such an enjoyable one. My thanks also to the distinguished author, Michael Arditti, for reading out the winning entry at the awards evening, and for speaking so helpfully and generously about the process of writing and becoming an author. I appreciate more than a little all the help I have had from the University of Chester's Corporate Communications team, especially Jayne Dodgson and Jenni Westcott. Without their patience and good-humoured support and advice, I might have floundered long ago. Sarah Griffiths as managing editor for the University of Chester Press has been wonderfully reassuring and helpful at each step of the way. I would like to thank Jennifer Bird and Emma Shipman from Learning and Information Services for capturing much of the spirit of *Patches of Light* in their very fine cover image.

    Finally, my infinite thanks to the authors themselves. It has been a privilege to work with you, and I have enjoyed and learnt from your stories.

Ian Seed
Chair Judging Panel, and Editor, *Patches of Light*,
Department of English, University of Chester,
May 2016

TICK TOCK

Pauline Brown

Pandora wants to be Jodie. Jodie's hair hangs in two rope plaits that are shiny and the colour of a bonfire. Like Princess Anna's hair before Elsa froze her heart. But Pandora knows that no amount of wishing or wanting will put her inside Jodie's body. So she has made Jodie her best friend instead. She has unpeeled the stickers from the wall above her bed, smoothed out their curled-up corners, and will give them to Jodie after school. Then Jodie will say that Pandora is her best friend too.

Jodie gets lots of attention. From everybody, but especially from the grown-ups. Mr Timpson didn't even tell her off when she tried to carve a bad word on her desk. He just took the scissors and locked them in his drawer, then carried on showing everyone how to make their bean seeds sprout, while Jodie sat in the play corner so Miss Hopkins could read her a story. And last weekend, Pandora's mum put some pasta bake into an old ice cream tub, and they took it round for Jodie's tea. Pandora went with Jodie to her bedroom, where they pretended to watch a DVD. But really they had rolled back the rug, and were lying with their ears pressed to the floorboards, listening to Jodie's mum wailing in the kitchen underneath. Jodie said it was because her stepdad had been told he couldn't live there any more. He wasn't even allowed to come back for his socks. At least not until after *the case*, and then it would *depend*. Jodie said her real dad might have to come home now, because otherwise her mum couldn't see how ends would ever meet.

'What should I call you?' the lady who is watching Pandora do her picture wants to know. The lady says her name is Wendy, just like Peter Pan's friend, and she is sitting ever so close, because, she says, she wants to be Pandora's friend too. But she isn't like the lady who came to see Jodie. Jodie's lady had purple shoes and sunglasses, and came to their school in a yellow car. This one came on a bicycle. Her shoes are flat, with laces, and her breath smells of breakfast.

Pandora's mum has promised chocolate milk at teatime, provided Pandora doesn't *indulge any fantasies* today. There might also be a *Frozen* duvet set waiting for a very good girl. Pandora is not sure exactly how good that means she must be, because ever since Kev came to live with them, she's been getting lots of things without trying hardly at all. Her mum pretends it's because Kev earns loads of money, so they can afford all that stuff now. But Pandora knows she just says this to make her *be nice to Kev*, and stop *going on* about her dad all the time.

'Do you have a nickname? Dora, perhaps?'

Pandora gazes at the cornflake-coloured wedge that is stuck between the front teeth of Wendy's smile. She wonders if she should mention it. But Miss Hopkins is over there on the other side of the table, and she hasn't said anything. Perhaps reminding people they should clean their teeth after breakfast is rude, even if it is for their own good.

'Or Pansy? Pansies are pretty.'

Pandora turns back to her picture to colour the trunk of her tree. Plain brown for now, but next she will use the orange crayon to add lots of squiggles. Then it will look like the real bark of the real tree that grows outside her bedroom window. She tilts her chair on to its front legs, and bends her head so that the tip of her nose is almost touching the paper. She likes the whispering sound her hair makes as it strokes her picture. Of course, she knows who Wendy is waiting for her to draw.

'You may call me Pandora.'

She would like to put snow on her tree and on the roof of her house. And all over Kev's dog, so that people will see she has frozen it – right there, in front of the garden gate. But snow is white and this paper Wendy has brought is white too. It was easy when she did her painting yesterday, because Mr Timpson said Jodie could give out the paper, which meant Pandora got blue.

She kneels up on her chair and throws her head back to study her tree. No matter if she cannot do snow, her branches shall have icicles instead. She takes a grey crayon from the box – because grey is almost the same as silver – and draws a long point, like a sword hanging down beside the ice blue curtains of her bedroom.

Wendy isn't watching. Instead she is frowning at the clock. Pandora frowns up at it too. She can sometimes tell the time now, but this clock is one of those with a red stick that won't keep still long enough for her to make up her mind. It can't be playtime yet, because nobody's outside making a racket. But Wendy has started to fidget. Her legs cross and uncross, as if she could *use a coffee*. Or maybe it's the toilet she needs. Either way, she's not paying attention. Pandora clamps her crayon in her fist and, pressing down as hard as she can, draws loud, angry icicles all over her tree. She feels the crayon snap in the palm of her hand.

'How about putting some more people into this lovely picture of yours?' Wendy may be looking again, but her voice sounds as if it's swallowing a yawn. 'Your mummy, perhaps.'

Pandora's broken crayon is still held together by its paper sleeve. The top half wobbles as she draws the outline of her sharpest, deadliest icicle yet. 'My mum is not there,' she says.

There, that's got Wendy's interest back. Her chair creaks, and her hand slides on to the table. Fluff from her cardigan crackles over Pandora's arm, making all the little white hairs stand up.

'Where has Mummy gone, Pandora? Will she be long?'

Tick Tock

Pandora thinks she can smell boiled egg, as well as the cornflakes. 'She's in the headmistress's office, of course. Waiting for us to finish in here. Didn't they tell you?'

Wendy flumps back in her seat. On the other side of the table, Miss Hopkins leans forward. 'What about you, Pandora? Aren't you going to be in your picture?'

'I'm there already. You just can't see me because I'm in bed, and my bed is under the window.' Silly Miss Hopkins should know this. She was there when Pandora painted her picture yesterday. Apart from the paper, and crayons instead of paints, this one will be almost the same.

Pandora picks up the green crayon she wants to use for her brother. Between him and Kev's dog she draws a lead. Now both of them are walking away from the house, with Toby's scarf sticking out behind him in the wind. In a moment she'll do the postman. Have him wave to Toby from his van.

'Is that Kevin there, taking the dog for a walk?' Wendy asks.

'No, it's my brother. And he isn't going for a walk. He's off to see our dad.'

She has only added this last bit because it seemed like a chance *to contradict*. But Pandora is worried now. She hadn't planned that Toby would be going to their dad's. When he arrives, *The Others* will be there too, and everyone will play in the garden and throw snowballs. What if they make a snowman and someone says they should call him Olaf? Her skin feels hot and a pillow fight is happening in her tummy again. If only she had made it rain. They would all have had to stay indoors and get bored. That would have served everyone right. She wonders if she could ask for a new piece of paper. But Wendy is looking at the clock again, and the clock's red stick is ticking away. Chairs are scraping the floor in the classroom next door. Any moment now, Wendy might gather her things and head for the staff room. Or climb on to her bicycle and set off for home.

Hurry now, Pandora. Be quick. But what colour to choose? What colour to use for Kev?

She takes the red crayon in her fingers and curves her arm around her picture. Bends her head low so that no one will see until she, Pandora, is ready. Her hair strokes the paper, whispering through the branches of her tree, snaking across the frozen pane of her window and over the ice blue of her curtains.

Pandora drops her crayon, tosses back her hair, pushes her chair away from the table.

And, oh, the look on Wendy's face. If only Jodie could see it too.

PURDY

Andrew Fleming

It was the first warm day of spring. I decided to dust off the bikes and see if Purdy wanted to come on a ride with me. To my surprise, Purdy – normally happier to stay at home with her toys and books – needed little persuasion. As I cleaned the last of the cobwebs from the handlebars, Susan helped her button up her coat and fasten her helmet.

'Are you sure you don't want to come too?' I asked Susan.

She shook her head and smiled. 'It'll be nice for you and Purdy to do something together. Just the two of you.'

Susan was right. I couldn't remember the last time I had spent any time with Purdy, and it felt good to be riding off down the street with her side by side. We made our way through the estate, past neighbours mowing their lawns and washing their cars, towards the country park on the edge of town. As we crossed the bridge that marked the park's entrance, I let Purdy ride in front of me, warning her with a ring of my bell when she got too far ahead. She was a sensible girl and a good cyclist, but the park was busy and I was anxious not to let her out of my sight.

Patches of Light

We took the path that circled the artificial lake. Ducks and moorhens drifted across the grey-green water, occasionally dipping their heads into the murk in search of food. Purdy wanted to stop and watch birds but I told her to keep riding.

'Where are we going, Daddy?' she asked over her shoulder.

'Eyes forward!' I shouted as Purdy veered towards an oncoming dog-walker.

She giggled and deftly steered her bike around a startled-looking Border collie.

On the far side of the lake, I told Purdy to turn on to the quieter track that led down through the woods to where the bluebells grew. But the track was muddy and uneven after the winter, and riding was fast becoming a chore. In front of me I saw Purdy slow down almost to a stop.

'Come on, Purd,' I said as I caught up with her, 'just a little bit further, then we can have a rest.'

'Something's wrong,' she said, frowning beneath the peak of her helmet.

I glanced at her bike and saw that her front tyre was flat. 'Looks like you've got a puncture, sweetheart. We'll have to stop and fix it.'

Leaning the bikes against a tree, I examined Purdy's tyre and soon found a small nail stuck at an angle into the rubber. I took out the spanner and puncture repair kit I kept in my pannier and set to work.

Purdy

Purdy sat down on a nearby log and watched as I removed the wheel then levered the tyre off the frame. I held the inner tube up to my ear and squeezed it, listening for the hiss of escaping air.

'What are you doing?' she asked.

'I'm looking for the hole inside your tyre so I can fix it.'

'Will it take long?'

'Just a few minutes.'

Purdy sighed. 'Daddy?' she said in the lilting tone she used when she wanted something. 'Can I have a new bike for my birthday?'

'What do you need a new bike for? There's nothing wrong with this one.'

'The tyre's broken.'

'It's not broken, it's just got a little hole in it,' I said, finally locating the source of the puncture. 'All I need to do is glue this patch on and it'll be as good as new in no time.'

'I'm too big for that bike now,' she said, trying a different tack.

'Then I'll raise the seat for you. Bicycles are expensive, Purdy. We'll buy you a new one when you really need it.'

I heard her kick a stone away in frustration.

'Maybe my real Mummy and Daddy could buy it for me?' She elongated the word *real*, knowing exactly where the power in her question lay.

I stopped – glue in one hand, inner tube in the other – and turned to face Purdy.

'Sweetheart,' I said, trying to keep my voice steady, 'what have we told you?'

Susan and I had never tried to hide the fact from Purdy that she was not our biological child, but neither did we encourage her to talk about it. She was our daughter now, and we didn't want her unsettled by thoughts of her old life.

'There's a girl in my class who's adopted and her real parents still—'

'Purdy!' I snapped. *'We're* your real parents.'

She stared at me, shocked by the harshness of my tone. Now she was getting older, perhaps it was only natural that she should start asking questions about her past. But I was worried what that would do to Purdy. I was worried what it would do to Susan.

'I know, Daddy,' she said quietly, 'I just ...'

I put the tyre down and sat on the log next to Purdy. I wrapped my arm around her narrow shoulders. 'I'm sorry. I didn't mean to shout at you.'

She avoided my eyes, focusing instead on digging a shallow trench with the toe of her shoe. 'I know I can't live with my old Mummy and Daddy any more. I just miss them sometimes.'

When Susan and I were first married, we had tried to have our own children. We saw doctor after doctor, tried every kind of fertility treatment, all to no avail. Eventually I had to face the fact that I would never be able to give Susan the child she so desperately wanted. It stretched our relationship to breaking point. I thought I was going to lose her.

Purdy

And then Purdy came into our lives. At first I wasn't sure we were doing the right thing, taking on a child in Purdy's situation. I knew it would be hard for all of us, but I also knew it would give Susan the chance to be the wonderful mother she always knew she could be. And so it proved. Purdy not only turned us into a family, she saved our marriage.

'You haven't talked about this to Mummy, have you?' I asked.

Purdy shook her head.

'Good girl. Because you know how much it would upset Mummy, don't you?'

'But why, Daddy?'

'Because we love you, Purdy. We love you much more than your old Mummy and Daddy did. We would never let you go, now, would we?'

She looked up at me and I could see the hurt in her eyes that my words were causing.

'Think about it,' I continued. 'You wouldn't be living with us in the first place if they'd loved you like we do. That makes sense, doesn't it?'

Purdy nodded slowly.

'So when you talk about them like that, calling them your real parents, it makes Mummy very unhappy. It makes her feel like you don't really love her. Like you're not grateful for what she's done for you. And that's not true, is it, Purdy?'

'No,' she whispered. 'I love Mummy.'

'Of course you do. We both do.' I squeezed her shoulder. 'Tell you what, maybe we'll buy you that new bike for your birthday after all. I hadn't realised how grown-up you were getting.'

I smiled at Purdy and she smiled back, pleased by the idea that she was a big girl now.

'Right,' I said as I picked up the tyre, 'give me two minutes and we'll be on our way.' I glued the patch over the hole in the inner tube and pressed hard until it held fast.

Waiting for the glue to dry, I reflected that Purdy was indeed growing up. Maybe this would bring yet more questions about her past, but she would also soon be old enough to understand what being part of a family really meant. She would come to realise that there were some things that had to be kept hidden, even from those closest to us. Especially from those closest to us.

I pumped the air back into the tyre and fixed the wheel back on the bike, giving the spanner an extra turn just to make sure the wheel was attached securely.

'There you go,' I said, 'good as new.'

'Good as new,' she repeated.

Susan and I were lucky to have Purdy. We would never forget that. As I helped her back on to her bike, I looked into my daughter's deep brown eyes, so different to my own. I was taken back to that summer's day at the seaside when we had first seen her, alone outside the amusement arcade. I could still see the look on her face as we approached, a look that seemed to say she had been expecting us. I remembered how we had taken her gently by the hand, while above us the seagulls circled and cried in a clear blue sky.

THE TIME TRAVELLER'S DAUGHTER

Jan Kaneen

'No, it's gone,' I snapped, flat-lipped and antsy. As soon as I said it, I wished I'd said it more kindly.

She's nearly always waiting for me when I find myself back here, in the bland, monochrome future. She's the only one with a hint of colour and I do quite like talking to her really. She nodded, looking unsurprised. Well, she is an expert and she is from the future and it's not that surprising when you think about it, that time travel affects your memory.

We were in the white room. Her hair was piled into a grey froth on top of her futuristic head. She's old, I think, but it's hard to tell because her skin's immobile like she's super-controlled or holding something back. Future people don't emote much. Passion seems to have died out there. Everyone looks mildly sympathetic or slightly concerned. They never shout or get irritated, not like people from the past, like me.

They're very interested in time travel though. Whenever I arrive, they want all the answers. She asked me who the Prime Minister was. I got irritated. I was cross because she knows full well that I've travelled through endless phases recently, jumping through decades. How on earth was I meant to know?

The Time Traveller's Daughter

I was about to tell her how much I enjoy our chats by way of an apology, but I started slipping. The future was fragmenting into shards like the turning pieces of a kaleidoscope, switching from black and white to cobalt blue and buttercup yellow. That often happens when I'm slipping back. It wrong-footed me at first but I'm used to it now. It's beautiful.

When everything settles, I'm looking over the railings of a black and red ferry into the grey-green choppy sea. I look round for Granddad. I've travelled here before so I know he's about somewhere. The boat is pitching and the wind is whipping the waves into grey foam. Fine flecks of sea water spray up into my face smelling of salt and seagulls. I lick my lips. Granny and Mary will be in the rest rooms right at the bottom with the other landlubbers. They think they'll feel better down there but they never do. Granddad and I always stay up top because we've got sea-legs and Granddad says that watching the wind is the best way to keep hold of your kippers. Granddad was born on the Isle of Man. We go there often in the school holidays to stay with Mrs Brew or Aunty Marie on the big ferry from Birkenhead.

I look down to see what I'm wearing, knowing it will be my black, patent leather shoes and red woollen coat. Granny sewed a cat on to my left pocket, cut out of black velvet. I like to stroke it when I'm feeling tired. My furry hat is tied with strings that have white pompoms on the ends. We made them together, Granny and me, winding wool around a cardboard hoop.

'Granddad,' I call and there he is by my side, in his black overcoat. His dandelion clock hair is thin, showing pink skin underneath as it blows in the gathering gale.

'You never named owt did you, my love?' He nods, almost smiling at the growing swell, staring far out to sea. 'You know 'ow they take on if you name the things you shouldn't.'

'Course I didn't,' I say, a bit cross at the suggestion because I'm ten and not a baby, 'I know what you can and can't say when you're on the sea, Granddad.'

He's talking about the fairies. Manx fairies are different to Cheshire fairies, naughtier and quicker to take offence. You have to be careful what you say in case they blow up a squall to teach you your manners. At sea you mustn't whistle or say 'rat' or 'cat', you have to say long-tailed fellow or scratchet and you mustn't ever say 'fairy', you have to say mooinjer veggey because that's Manx for little people and it's full of respect.

'What'll we do to pass the time?' he asks. 'Spin the yarn of Mananon's Cloak or spit bubbles into the foam?' He knows I'll say bubbles.

No other grown-up ever allows spitting and no-one can spit like Granddad, not me, not my sister, not my Gran and we've all tried and tried, well except for Granny who's from Frodsham. They don't spit in Frodsham. It's not ladylike. I look at Granddad, getting his tongue into the right shape, folding it down the middle lengthways so it's rolled tight and pointed at the end. He scoops up some silvery spit that's been pooling underneath. When it's on the tip of his tongue he blows very, very gently until a bit of breath fills up the spit. That's as far as I can get, making the bubble, but I can't set it free, not yet, so I give up. Granddad's bobbles about in the gale then disappears against the darkening sky. I give Granddad a round of applause but I have to stop almost straightaway because the boat is lurching downward and I have to hold on to the railings. As we dip right down, the sky becomes all sea and the seagull cries change shape so I know that I'm time-travelling again. I don't mind. I expect I'll be back one day.

'Mummy, Mum, Mother,' I hear Abbey's far distant voice calling me, sad like seagulls as the boat tips back. I shoot through time and space toward her.

I came to time travel late in life. I don't recall ever doing it before Edward died. I certainly never did when Abbey was growing up. Maybe it was grief that triggered it off; how long were we married? Thirty, fifty years … though I doubt it. I've always been very resilient like that, tough as old boots.

'Are you there, Abbey?' I call back, looking at the whitened sky. I'm outside the playground waiting for her I think. The horse chestnut tree is laden with clusters that prick the watercolour clouds. I remember that it's autumn and Abbey is about ten, though she looks much older.

She says, 'I thought you were never coming back, Mum.'

'What a silly,' I say, 'don't I collect you every day?' Her hopeful smile flattens. Her ammonite eyes that look like mine, that look like Granddad's, dampen.

She says, 'What day is it, Mum?' I'm just about to say it's Funday because that's what I always say when we go for a jolly to Grosvenor Park, or to feed the ducks, or have a picnic and because I know she'll be afraid and upset if she realises that her Mother has no idea what day it is, but I start slipping again, much too soon.

When everything settles, I'm lying on the bottom bunk in the dark morning, snug and warm. I don't know I'm four. Father is standing up so I can't see his face.

'I am just going to say it because there is no easy way of telling you thi—' His control cracks, like someone stole the end of his sentence. He's talking to my sister on the top bunk because she's six and she knows she is.

'Your Mother is dead.' I can tell by his knees that he's crying silently and that he's hugging her. After a while he kneels. 'Did you hear me, Elizabeth?' He's looking at my dry eyes. 'Your Mother is dead.'

I nod.

The Time Traveller's Daughter

He stands up again. 'She doesn't understand,' he says to Mary, 'she's too little.'

Time travel can be upsetting sometimes when you go somewhere you'd rather not be but I don't stay anywhere for long these days. I'm glad when it melts away.

Back in the future I wiped my eyes. She was crouching by my side, next to the chair I seemed to be sitting in, reading my face,

'Are you ok?' she asked. I was surprised to see that the future had brightened, not much though, into muted pastels, only just colours. 'Do you really not know?'

I looked at her touch on my tiny, sparrow-claw hand wondering how it had grown so old. I had that feeling you get when you go into a room to fetch something but forget what it is you went in for. She looked so familiar – that stone-grey stare. I scratched my head as if that would help. It was on the tip of my tongue.

'Did I used to know you?' I said.

She rolled her lips together tight over her teeth and turned away. I didn't hear her reply because the future had fragmented, letting brighter colours in.

I could hear Abbey calling, 'Mother, Mum, it's me,' from her wedding day. I love travelling back here. Eddie's smiling so proud in his dove grey top hat, giving her away, in the buttercup sunshine and the scent of roses.

WATER WORLD

Sue Hoffmann

'Marnie Watson! Get your hands out of that tank!'

Marnie stepped back guiltily, shaking water from her fingers.

'What have I told you, Marnie?' her mother demanded. 'That's not good for you or the fish.'

'Sorry,' mumbled Marnie, but she wasn't really. She just couldn't help it. She'd tried to explain it to Mum but had failed miserably. The words had sounded odd, even to Marnie.

She waited until her mother was busy with a customer, then crept towards one of the large tanks at the rear of the shop. Nose pressed against the glass, she watched, spellbound, as two peppered catfish bumbled their way across the gravel, barbels probing for tiny morsels of food. A shoal of neon tetras swirled in front of her eyes, flashing their patriotic colours in a dazzling display. A lone platy darted in to disturb the neons and they fled to the refuge of the sunken wreck in the corner of the tank.

Marnie felt sorry for the little platy. Its two companions had been bought just yesterday and Marnie was convinced the one left behind was searching for its friends. Many times she had seen her mother take fish from quarantine and add them to a display tank, and invariably they went to others of their own kind. The platy was lonely. If only she could make the neons understand, perhaps they would play with it until more platies arrived or it was sold.

Though Marnie knew *Water World* was a business and her parents needed to make money, she was always sad to see any of the fish leave the shop. She'd heard that people who sold dogs and cats often made home checks to ensure the animals were going to be cared for properly. Why didn't her parents do that for the fish? Fish were creatures too. Surely they had as much right as cats and dogs to be looked after correctly.

Tearing herself away from the emerging neons and the desolate platy, Marnie moved across to the next tank. She liked this kind of display best. The marine fish were so colourful, so varied, she never tired of looking at them. She glanced over to check that her mother was still busy, then stood on tiptoe and dabbled her fingers in the water. Salt. It took all her willpower not to put her hand to her mouth and suck her fingers.

An orange clownfish wiggled over to investigate the pink, wormy things invading the surface of its domain. Marnie giggled as it tickled the tip of her middle finger.

'Marnie. Marine,' she chanted softly. 'Marine. Marnie.'

Approaching footsteps alerted her to her mother's presence, and Marnie took her hand out of the water just in time.

Patches of Light

'Lunch, Marnie,' her mother said. 'Go and wash your hands.'

Marnie trotted off to the private rooms at the back of the shop. Obediently, she scrubbed her hands before sitting down to eat her sandwich. The bread was fresh and the egg filling tasty, but Marnie struggled to force it down. Dad was due back with new stock and he'd promised to let Marnie choose the layout of a tank ready for when the fish went on display in the shop. She was too excited to eat.

Ideas swirled in her head, bumbling around like the catfish. Should she have a shipwreck model? No, there was already one in the neons' tank. What about a fairy tale castle? No again; that wouldn't look real. There were no castles under the sea, were there? The tank would be for marine fish and Marnie wanted it to look like their real home in the sea so that they wouldn't be homesick. Dad said the fish were bred here, not caught from the wild, but Marnie was sure they'd know the difference between a castle and a coral reef.

A coral reef. That was it. There were plenty of model reefs from which to choose, but she knew that 'live' rock and sand were best for marine fish. And salt, of course. Dad used *Ocean Waves* salt, so Marnie would use that, too. Dad would help her mix it, and he'd sort out the lighting and heating and the filters for her – but she could select the plants and, most important of all, the fish. She'd learned which ones could live safely together and which needed to be

Water World

kept separate. Dad would put them in the tank for her and check her choices, but Marnie was sure she wouldn't make any mistakes.

'Have you finished, Marnie?' her mum called from just inside the shop. 'Put your plate in the sink, and go and do your homework.'

Marnie hurried to do as she was told. She wanted to be ready for when Dad came home. Fortunately, there wasn't much to do – just some handwriting practice to complete. She'd learnt her spellings and done her number work last evening so that she would have Saturday free.

She heard Dad's van draw up in the yard and ran to the back door to meet him.

It had been the best day yet. Marnie pulled the bedclothes up to her chin and snuggled down, savouring the memory of setting up the tank with Dad. It had to stand for a while, Dad said, but it would look wonderful once the fish were in. Marnie wanted to drift off to sleep and dream about swimming with the fish in the tank, but she was suddenly very thirsty. She pushed back the covers and thrust her feet into her slippers – and almost fell over as she tried to walk. Looking down, she saw that she had put both feet into one slipper. She sat on the edge of her bed and put her slippers on properly before heading to the bathroom for a drink of water.

Her parents' bedroom door was ajar and she could hear her mother saying, 'Vicky Barnes came into the shop today. Her baby's due next week.'

Marnie stopped to listen.

'Did Marnie say anything?' Dad asked.

'No, but I thought she was going to.'

'Well,' Dad said, 'she knows she's adopted and she knows how special she is to us. I don't think seeing Vicky will set off more questions about babies.'

'What if she does ask?' Mum said.

'About her birth mother? She's only seven, Karen. I don't think she'll worry about that until she's a bit older.'

'She's a very clever seven, Steve. She'll want to know.'

'And we'll tell her the truth – when she's ready to hear it.'

Marnie's mum's voice rose. 'Tell her? Tell her she was abandoned on a beach and found by a man walking his dog?'

On a beach? Marnie stood, transfixed. She wasn't upset. In fact, she was quite pleased. Maybe that was the reason she liked sea creatures so much.

She heard movement and darted off to the bathroom before her mum or dad came out of their bedroom. It would never do to be caught listening outside the door.

Marnie filled a glass with water and put it ready on the bathroom stool. On impulse, she put the plug

Water World

into the washbasin and turned on the cold tap until the basin was half-full, then she dipped both hands into the water, relishing the chill and the wetness. She stared hard at her hands.

'Are you all right, Marnie?' her mum asked.

Marnie turned round. She hadn't heard her mother come into the bathroom.

'Yes, Mum,' she said, pulling the plug to let the water drain. She wiped her hands on her towel and picked up the glass of water.

'Back to bed, then,' her dad said from the doorway.

Her parents followed her into her bedroom. Mum took the glass and put it on the bedside table while Dad tucked her in. 'Goodnight, my little mermaid,' he said, kissing her on the forehead.

Marnie smiled. She liked that nickname. 'Dad,' she said, 'can I show you something?'

'It's late, Marnie,' her mother said. 'Can't it wait until tomorrow?'

'I suppose so,' Marnie agreed.

'Right,' her Dad said. 'Tomorrow it is. You can show both of us then.'

He and her mum left the room, closing the door behind them. Marnie didn't mind the dark, but she wanted to have another look so she waited a few minutes and then switched on the bedside lamp.

Yes. She *was* right. Her hands had definitely changed. The webbing between the fingers was now quite distinct, and those funny marks on her sides looked just like the gills on the fish. She wondered if her parents would be pleased or cross.

Reaching out, she picked up the glass of water, added some pilfered *Ocean Waves* salt, stirred it with her finger and drank it in one long gulp.

THE SWIMMING POOL

Liz Milne

The swimming pool was calm and ripple-free; the large natatorium deserted but for the slender lifeguard moving slowly, sweeping the puddles left by the previous swimmers (a lively gaggle of schoolchildren) into the drains set at regular intervals around the bath. Recreational swim started at twelve and the regulars would arrive soon.

Marge – short for Margaret, but she much preferred the snappy soubriquet used by her young, hip classmates – whisked her towel from around her waist and walked to the poolside. She lowered herself into the water, sighing with relief as the kindly water closed over her bulgy hips and bottom. Happier, she moved to the side of the pool that benefited from a long, narrow strip of sunshine. She kicked off vigorously, moving easily into the strong breaststroke that she could keep up for ages.

Marge had the pool to herself for a time. She delighted in gliding along, looking up at the underside of the water, seeing small specks of dust and detritus magnified there, anchored into the meniscus like prehistoric creatures in tar pits. She relished the thrust generated by the kick of her legs and the pull of the muscles in her arms and shoulders.

Patches of Light

Steve – never Steven, always just Steve – hastened out of the men's changing room, glancing hopefully at the water as he settled his goggles over the tight clench of his swimming cap. Just one other person there, he noted without really registering the thought. It was hard to tell anything else about her: a sleek silver cap snugged down over her head and expensive goggles covered her eyes. She could be almost anyone. He shrugged off thoughts of his pool companion and concentrated on fastening on the arm and leg weights that he used to strengthen his muscles and build stamina. After a cautious length of freestyle by way of warm-up, he burst into an explosive butterfly, churning his way down the lane and back again.

Marge, still forging her way along her sunshine path, took in every detail of the young man as he came out of the changing room.

'Mmm,' she thought to herself, grinning. She angled her face into the water so he could not see it. She was old enough to know better, she was probably old enough to be his mother! He was … old enough to be fair game anyway! No! Behave, Marge! She swam on, occasionally casting mildly lustful glances at the young man as he thrashed back and forth, his well-muscled body displacing the water in choppy wavelets that broke the smooth water surface.

Steve sped from one end of the pool to the other and back. He switched smoothly from butterfly to

The Swimming Pool

backstroke to freestyle, using weights, flippers and hand-paddles to increase his water resistance. As he settled into his regimen he allowed his mind to wander. He wondered, was she a secretary? Faculty? A mature student, perhaps? He could not tell what age she was precisely. She was definitely over thirty, but beyond that he could not tell: goggles and swimming caps had the effect of making everyone look similar, with minor variations on a size and shape theme.

As the lifeguard stepped around the pool, finally putting her wide broom away, Steve's attention moved to her. She was his age: early twenties, he estimated. Her wide-set eyes were mistrustful and visibly blue. Her hair was clean and shiny, a uniform black that spoke of dye. She was wearing a bright yellow t-shirt, as did all the lifeguards, but she wore jogger bottoms rather than the customary shorts. As he swam towards her, Steve studied her, wondering about the aberrant trousers. His eyes followed her movements as she pushed her short sleeve up to scratch absent-mindedly at her upper arm. The colourful swirl of a tattoo peeked out from under the cheerful yellow fabric. That was it! She must have tattoos on her legs that would be revealed by the hemline of the shorts: hence the trousers. As he neared the pool edge, she stepped toward him, bending to pick up a piece of litter. This unexpected proximity revealed a neat metallic gleam along the delicate curve of her ear, a row of piercings counterpointed by an eyebrow bar and the discreet twinkle of a nose stud. Steve found himself intrigued: tattoos and piercings were not often found on the poolside.

Cara straightened, carrying the litter to the nearby dustbin between two fingers. Dropping it in and wiping her fingers on her trousers, she stifled a yawn and walked around the pool, hoping that movement would keep her attentive. As she walked at a measured pace, she considered the two pool users. She had seen the boy before, often. He was constantly in the pool, flexing his muscles. He might be quite nice, if only he would reveal a hint of his real self. She was sure that there must be something beneath that perfect exterior – some intelligence, humour or, hell, even darkness – something to show that he was not just a glossy shell. Cara watched the woman for a moment, feeling an unwilling admiration for her steady and almost stately progress. As she continued to walk around the pool, she pondered the calm and tranquil atmosphere of the natatorium. It was a far remove from the rave she had attended the night before: the strobing lights, the heaving crowd a single, many-headed creature; noise a tangible throbbing and pulsing, blessedly driving out rational thought.

Cara sat down for a few moments on the bench by the pool, her eyes following Steve's progress. He was beginning to tire now, his sleek movements becoming laboured and his breathing shortening.

The Swimming Pool

Cara ran her hands over her head, feeling the roughness of the black dye but relishing her new look. As soon as her shift was over she would be back in her new, stiff black clothing – a defensive barrier between her and the rest of the world. Just one year before, one year? Was that all? She had been blonde and pretty and perfect on the outside, but completely hollow on the inside. No substance. Nothing real. All appearance, nothing else … It was better now.

Steve *was* tiring. He could feel his strength draining away with each successive lap and he gritted his teeth, pushing himself to complete his regimen. The doctor had recommended swimming as a way to build up his stamina after his illness. Just one year before, one short year, he had been a weedy, knock-kneed weakling. No breath, no muscle tone, no chance. Now look at him, a survivor. The new treatment had worked, against the odds, and he was poised on the brink of his life. A life suspended for a while, about to be curtailed and now stretching before him once again. And this time he would make the most of it.

Marge decided to swim four more lengths before calling time. She enjoyed her daily half hour, she liked to call it her therapy. Her body took care of the swimming, leaving her brain free to meander in any direction it chose. Story ideas, essay plans, even new recipes and holiday destinations all neatly organised while she swam. Just one year before, one packed year, she had been a frustrated housewife, watching her children growing up and away from her, seeing her job pool dwindling into dull secretarial boredom or – worse – bookkeeperly ennui. In a fit of frustration she had applied to university, dusting off long-suppressed ambitions and hopes. The first enthralling year was almost over and she was anticipating the long vacation before the second year: the reading and writing necessary to plunge back into full-time academia. It was a matter of pride that almost every essay and assignment had come back with high marks and she was determined that her standards would not fall.

Marge dried herself and dressed quickly, having quickly jotted down a story idea that had occurred to her as she swam, as so often happened. She ran a comb through her hair, packed her swimming things away and headed out.

Steve dried off slowly, sitting on a bench, relishing the heaviness of tired muscle as the towel see-sawed across his broad shoulders. He dressed with meticulous care, paying careful attention to drying between his toes. His brush with death had infused him with a certain self-interest that manifested as exquisite attention to his physical well-being. Finally ready, he glanced at his watch and ascertained that it was lunch-time. He set off.

Cara swept around the poolside one final time before she pulled the heavy cover across the water, fixing it into place deftly. She walked around double-checking that all was neat and tidy. Satisfied, she

The Swimming Pool

headed into the staff changing room and dressed herself, ceremonially donning the long black clothes and applying dark eye-shadow and black lipstick. She lingered for a moment, looking out into the tranquil space that housed the pool.

Then she switched off the lights and left the building.

HONEY FOR THE BAG LADY

Valentine Williams

Her bag wasn't in its usual place, Sarah noticed. It was a large, well-made leather bag containing a quantity of pockets and zipped compartments. The cat was sitting on top of it, pretending to be asleep, but Sarah could see one yellow eye squinting at her, half-open.

'Off!' she cried, furious, pulling the long black strap away from the chair. The cat pretended it had been about to move anyway and descended from the chair with dignity. The bag was covered in cat hair. Sarah grabbed it and rummaged in the outside pockets for her travel pass. No luck. The cat gave her an insolent look and sauntered to the door. Where was her travel pass? Might it have dropped inside the bag?

Sarah thrust her hand deep into the bag and was startled that her hand went in right up to the elbow. And there was still no sign of the pass. Her fingers touched something else; something she did not recognise. It felt greasy and brittle. A piece broke off in her hand and she pulled it out. There was a smell of beeswax and honey.

'Rob, can you come here a moment?'

'Problem?' He wasn't really interested; Sarah was always losing things or wanting something fixing.

Honey for the Bag Lady

'Look. I just pulled this out of my handbag.' She held out the fragment of honeycomb. He looked at it suspiciously. It was sticky.

'Out of your bag? How on earth could it have got in there?'

Sarah's eyebrows went up.

'I don't know. I put my hand into my bag to find my travel pass, and then I pulled this out. There's more of it in there. Can you look inside it for me?'

He put his ear to the bag. There was a quiet humming in the depths. The cat was watching them from the cat flap, ready to exit quickly.

'You must have left it somewhere outside, for a bee to get in. I'll empty it in the garden, so whatever's in there can fly away.'

'Thanks.'

He took the bag gingerly, holding it closed. It wasn't large enough to contain a whole honeycomb, surely? It was, he reckoned, about 25 centimetres in depth. She was lucky whatever was in the bag hadn't stung her. He held it upside down over the concrete flags of the patio and shook it. The cat watched from a safe distance, sceptically. But nothing came out. He shook it again. Nothing happened. Still he could hear faint buzzing. He tried to open the neck of the bag a little wider so he could see inside. Pinpricks of light flashed in the depths of the bag. The humming ceased. He nearly put his hand in, then changed his mind.

Patches of Light

'Got a torch?' he shouted. 'Bring me that torch that's under the sink, can you?'

'What have you found? Anything?'

'Nothing came out when I shook it.'

'Have you put your hand inside?'

'No. And I'm not going to.' If this was some horrible joke or trick he'd be really angry. Sarah found the torch. He held the bag open while she shone the torch inside. Tiny pin pricks of light moved around in the darkness.

'There's something in there moving.'

'What is it? Can you see?'

The tiny lights retreated to the bottom of the bag and slowly went out. Then the bag gave a slight squirm in his hands and he almost dropped it.

'I'm going to take the bag and dump it in the deep freeze. That should sort it out. Show me that piece you pulled out, the one you showed me.'

But Sarah couldn't find it. She'd put it on the table, she was sure she had. Maybe the cat, who had come indoors again, had knocked it off.

'I don't know what happened to it.'

'Oh for heaven's sake, Sarah.' He fetched a bamboo cane from the flowerbed and pushed it into the bag. He stopped when the cane kept on going and his hand became dangerously close to the opening. 'This is crazy. Your bag isn't that deep.'

'I know.'

The neck of the bag twitched. A bee squeezed through the gap and flew off, followed by another

Honey for the Bag Lady

bee, and another. A stream of bees flew off towards the garden. The cat's eyes moved sideways and back, following them. The bees vanished in the next garden.

'I'm glad they left,' said Sarah. 'I hope the bag's not all sticky inside.' She still hadn't found her travel pass, or her reading glasses, or the letter she had meant to post to her aunt. She had her purse, this time, in her shopping bag, but that was all.

Rob took the bag, holding it carefully by the strap and took it to the garage. He opened the freezer and dropped the bag inside. Cold steam escaped from the freezer; he was grateful for it. Whatever was in the bag could turn to ice for all he cared.

He banged the lid down harder than he meant to. A faint noise came from inside the cabinet. He ignored it; it was most likely ice dislodged from the lid or something. If Sarah wasn't such a slut it would have been defrosted properly and the contents properly labelled and stored, instead of them being dumped in the bottom in various bags and boxes. They'd bought the freezer from a friend whose shop was closing down. A sticky residue of ice-cream carton bases still lingered in the cold metallic corners. The bag, he imagined, would soon be stuck to the base as well.

Maybe he should get it out and have a look? Had he really seen tiny lights inside it?

The cat jumped up on to the lid and looked at him, questioningly. He pushed it off. Sarah found her travel pass in her jacket pocket and held it up to show him:

'You'll never guess where I found it! By the way, how long do you think I need to keep my bag in the freezer?'

'Overnight should do it. Where are you going?'

'Just round to see Celia. You'll be okay?'

'I'll have to be,' he said grumpily. 'You give me no choice.' Sarah sighed and gave him a false smile as she left. He felt suddenly bereft. In the living room he dozed off in front of the TV, then got up and made himself some supper, before realising that Sarah wasn't back. He thought about the black leather bag still in the freezer. Did he need to wait until morning to get it out? He unlocked the side door into the garage and went to the freezer. The cat jumped down from its perch on the window sill and followed him. He lifted the heavy white lid of the freezer slowly and peered inside. There wasn't a good light in the garage, but he could make out a dark stiff shape at the bottom, covered in ice crystals. The cat at his feet rubbed itself around his ankle. He pushed it away with his foot. He reached his arms in slowly and took hold of the bag; pulled it up and out of the freezer. The cat suddenly spat and gave a hiss and bolted for the open door to the house.

He handled the bag slowly, running his fingers along the zip. Then he undid it. He could hear Sarah's key in the lock.

'Hello? I'm home.'

Honey for the Bag Lady

'So I see.'

'What are you doing with my bag?'

'Looking to see what all the fuss was about.'

'And? What have you found out? What about the bees?'

'Oh, the bees. ... Here, see for yourself.' She approached cautiously. 'Don't worry, they'll all be frozen solid. That is, if there are any.'

'What do you mean? You saw them!'

'No darling, you saw them. You found that piece of honeycomb that disappeared. Remember? You really think there were bees in your bag?'

Sarah began to cry. The cat looked sympathetically at her. Rob smiled and looked away. His foot crunched something sticky. Honeycomb.

THE HARVESTER

Laura Thompson

By the end of the year, my father and I are the only ones left. Our allotment, sealed off with sweetcorn, grows alone. Beryl used to own the one to the left of ours, but she gave up when each cut into her vegetables spilled rot on to her kitchen counters. The flies stayed for days, Beryl told me, a small shocked face beneath perfectly shaped white hair.

    She was the first one to arrive and the first one to leave. Well, first after my father and me. We have been gardening as long as I can recall. Every season, every day, my dad pulls earth from stubborn earth. His palms cradle dirt where they once cradled me. His vegetables are always the best, too. Year after year yielded Mr Harris, on the right, dead crops. And his scarecrow, Mr Harris said, his scarecrow was the reason. It was sabotage.

    Mr Harris was the one who led the charge against the young couple from the plot beyond his. A middle-aged, plum-shaped man, but something fierce with a spade in hand. No one liked the young couple, anyway. They weren't in it for the veg, that's what my dad always murmured to me. They were only interested in getting a chicken coop. When they didn't, they snapped the necks of all the other chickens on the plot and displayed the bodies,

The Harvester

dangling limp along their shed's lip like fairy lights. Mr Harris left soon after that, too.

But I am told not to worry about that. My dad and I have been gardening alone for a month now. Mr Harris lies under our gooseberry bushes but he weeps and so we cannot talk.

My dad says: 'Loneliness is that which gives our love meaning.'

But we have never been without each other.

Today, we harvest my favourite. Potatoes. Each turn of the soil is a surprise, each stab of the fork a gamble. Every so often my dad will raise it and find potatoes impaled like heads on Tower Bridge. He'll give an ancient warrior cry, shake the fork, a conqueror. The potatoes scream but can do nothing. Dad has been sweating these sticky slug-trails for decades. There is no escape.

I like the tiny ones. The barely formed creatures, the size of the tip of my finger. They remind me of my father's legs: thin and cold and pale. But they are absent today, much to my frustration. One of the snapped parsnips sits up and tells me that it saw the potatoes hiding behind our makeshift water collection and I drive my spade into its chalky flesh again and again and again.

My dad says: 'You never know what's beneath the slop and the suck of the mud.'

I start to respond, but then Beryl waves from the apple tree, pinned as she is by climbing vine weed. Beryl wanted to make love to the young couple. I think that was why she really left. The young couple cannot be found under any particular bush. They smile from behind the greenhouse and dance with our overgrown carrots. They will not talk to me.

Sometimes my dad stumbles when he digs. Sometimes I dig until I find the womb of the earth and I crawl back inside. Sometimes we curl up together in the soil and watch those limp chickens swing above us.

Beryl tells me not to worry. She tells me that everything we have ever been told is true.

As he digs, I crack the flat side of the spade on the back of my dad's head. He tumbles like a snapped sunflower. He falls and where he falls, I finally see. There are the potatoes. There, lying together, keeping still, keeping quiet. They hold each other close and, when I lay my father down with them, they hold him too.

MY WILL NE'ER BE DONE

Lynne Parry-Griffiths

Darkness pressing my eyes.
    Pushing, further, deeper.
    Cold. So cold.
    Darkness.

It was the smell. A foetid, dirt-tasting reek, unfamiliar in our age of baths and showers. Naked feet, spattered long shirt-sheet, Jesus-haired.

I have to be asleep. No one wakes up and sees a bewildered man standing out of time by their empty pillow, do they? Not unless they're really mad.

'You?'

He blinks, finger-rakes his hair from his face, as I always knew he would, scratches his scalp.

'Do you know where you are?'

Shakes that hair. It covers his shoulders.

'Do you know how you got here?'

'I was in my bed.'

His speech is alien, slow.

'Alone?'

He frowns.

'Darkness. Then cold.'

'I'll run you a bath. Warm you.'

'Run?'

I reach over, take his hand. The skin is soft, healed at last.

'I'll show you.'

He looks down at the fingers encasing his own, tightens.

'Where are you taking me?'

'Don't be frightened. You'll see.'

His odour envelops; once I would have recoiled, but with him it's some sort of comfort, the integral essence of his time. Leading him to the bathroom, I feel like an unfamiliar mother. He tenses in the atmosphere of tiles and porcelain, caught in someone else's dream.

'I'm going to put the light on. It'll be sudden, but your eyes will adjust.'

'Candles?'

'No. You ready?'

'For what?'

'This.' I pull on the cord, the bathroom explodes into existence. A different universe.

A sharp inhalation. I pat his arm.

'It's fine. You'll get used to it.'

His head turns, focussing.

'What is that seat?'

'The loo.'

Nothing.

'Where you, you relieve yourself?'

'A piss pot?'

It's my turn to smile. 'Sort of, but this lets you flush it away. You don't have to clear it out.' I raise the lid. 'You can sit or stand. And when you've finished, you press this button, here.'

My Will Ne'er Be Done

'This?' He points, presses, sends a flush into the bowl, it splashes upwards. Gasps, curses.

'It's alright.' I take his arm again. 'It's only flushing, it won't flood. The water takes away whatever's in the bowl.'

'Where?'

'To the sewers, and eventually the sea, I think.'

'And fish?'

I mustn't laugh.

'No, I promise it's safe. Now shall we get that bath sorted?'

Nods.

'You can wash your hair too.'

'Why?'

'I'll wash it for you, if you like.'

Eyes slide, catch. We are not children. He hasn't asked how we know each other.

'Have you a lice comb?'

'I think I can find one.' I won't tell him it belongs to the cat, hope head lice are his only parasite. I'll have to find him something to change into.

'Thank you.'

He watches me organise towels, bottles. Another exhalation as the taps are turned.

'I wish I could understand.'

I straighten, take his face in my hands, I don't have to stretch far.

'You will, but maybe not tonight.' Bend again to the bath.

'Do you not light a fire?'

'It heats itself.'
'Alchemy?'
'Not really.' I wave a bottle. 'You can wash with this. When you're ready, I'll do your hair.'

He tugs at his shirt, his calves are alabaster.

'I'll let you get undressed in peace. You turn the water off by twisting the taps, like this.' I show him, a sudden silence joins us.

'It has gone?'

'Do you want more?' The tub is less than half-full.

'There is more than enough. I will bathe, even though I probably do not need to.'

I cannot help myself.

'What have I said?'

'I'm sorry. I'll just be next door.'

I can hear him patting the water, laughing quietly, relishing the sensation of warm, clean water. He is a new child, a man who has never seen a tap, running water or even a bathroom. He is accepting, unquestioning, and neither of us is afraid.

When he wants, I will wash his hair, working the unctuous liquid through the knots of his scalp. I will scour and scrub, stop myself from reacting when the creatures move beneath my fingernails. When he is clean, I will spread conditioner between my palms, smooth the snare of curls.

My Will Ne'er Be Done

He is calling. I find a dressing-gown, hope it will cover most of him. He is not tall, probably undernourished, a slight gap between his teeth.

'Is everything OK?'

He will be frowning again.

'Are you well?'

'I am well.'

'Do you want me to wash your hair?'

'Thank you.'

Sitting in his water, he doesn't appear embarrassed. Soap is smeared around his shoulders and back. His skin is already cooling.

'Close your eyes. You don't want to get shampoo in them.'

'What is that?'

'What? Shampoo?'

'What tongue is that?'

'Not English, not originally anyway. I think it's Hindi, Sanskrit. It cleans your hair better than soap. I'll put conditioner on too.'

He has no idea what I mean, but nods, leans forward. Already he feels a part of this fabric.

Fingers circle in my hair, a not unpleasant sensation. She has become my mother. Tells me I must close my eyes, the liquid will hurt but I cannot see what she is doing, how she must be concentrating. I hope she will remove the lice.

Water trails over my skin, my face. I am glad to listen and keep my eyes fast. I cannot help but release.

She is speaking.

'Do you hear the clean? This conditioner might feel cold but I'll comb it through. When you're dry, I'll sort your, your ...'

She cannot tell me I am lousy.

I do all she asks. Stand in front of the large soft cloth she holds out, trying not to look or touch. I would not mind. I wrap the cloth about me, a loincloth or winding sheet, another figure of antiquity.

I drain his bath as he dries, the towel rasping. If we have a tomorrow I will buy him clothes, things he has never imagined. A hand towel about his shoulders catches the still dripping hair.

Even with the conditioner the curls are reluctant to part, perhaps I ought to have used olive oil. The bevel edge of the comb should lightly touch the scalp, be worked right through to the ends. His hair is dense, almost ringletted. Most women would be jealous of its texture. No grey threads are worked into its thick fabric. We forget he is still young.

Section, comb, wipe, rinse. Watch the microscopic insects strive against the white of the tissue paper, legs protesting. They cannot fly, but will crawl, stroll even, perhaps saunter, along individual strands of hair, biting their host's scalp, feeding, mating, reproducing.

It takes almost an hour. He's patient, more patient than I could ever be. This must be familiar, a routine he usually performs for himself. Sometimes the comb catches, snags, an involuntary inhalation, never complaining.

His hair has not fully dried by the time we are done and the bathroom has cooled. I don't know what time it is, it is still dark outside. I take his hand again, slow steps, toes curling into the softness of the carpet. I should have given him nail clippers. Take him to the guest bed, don't tell him it is always made up.

'Would you like to put the light on?'

'It will not burn?'

'No. Just press down on this.' I place his finger on the switch. 'That's it.'

Smiles, proud.

'It is bright.'

'Too bright?'

'Yes.'

I switch on the bedside lamp, tell him to touch the light switch again.

'How do you make the candle go out?'

'I don't.' Tomorrow may be packed with explanation. I push back the duvet, pat the mattress, say I hope he will be comfortable.

'Thank you.'

Patches of Light

'I'll leave you in peace. If you need to get up, it's the door at the top of the stairs.'
'There is no piss pot under the bed?'
'No. You press the button. Like I showed you?'
More magic.
'And the light will burn out by itself?'
'No. There is a switch, here.' I proffer a white rectangle, press down on it.

I do not know who or what I am. My eyes are heavy, weighted. I cannot move. They have tricked me, rewritten me. I am calling, calling, pleading for the light to come back.

And she is cradling me, my hair still wet against her, and I am weeping.

His bones are biting, but I won't let him go until he has calmed. Over and over, assure him he is safe here, in this now. I hope he believes me. Inhale his clean, his new-born, no, reborn, life. Together, we will inter that past, rest his ghosts, open a new page, and one day he will tell me the story, but for now, we will sleep.

CURSED

Gordon Williams

Kwanza asked me why I wanted the curse.

'It's a secret,' I told him. 'You won't tell anyone, will you?'

He smiled and looked at me, sitting on the bench outside his hut, chewing khat. 'Does your mother know you want the curse?' he asked.

'No, no – you mustn't tell her,' I said.

'How old are you now, Mkweli?' he asked, still smiling.

'Nearly fourteen,' I told him.

'Have you got a young man yet?' he asked. I felt my face burning. Why did he keep asking questions? I just wanted a curse setting, that was all. I shook my head.

'A pretty girl like you should have a young man,' he said and I could see his yellow teeth as he smiled. 'What will you give me for this curse – if I decide to set it for you?' He leaned over to put his hand on my shoulder but I moved away from him.

'Don't be frightened, Mkweli,' he said. 'There's no curse on you.'

'If I give you my silver bracelet – is that enough?' I asked him. He stopped smiling and his forehead became creased under his crinkly grey hair. He didn't say anything and I stood there waiting for him to answer. I couldn't leave Matumi in the field much longer on her own. Why couldn't he just say *yes* and do it?

'Come back tomorrow,' Kwanza said, spitting khat leaves on the ground, 'with your bracelet ... and a good reason for the curse.'

I couldn't wait any more; I told him I'd come back tomorrow and ran off to the field where Matumi was collecting groundnuts. She was squatting, next to a heap of nutshells on an old piece of blue cloth, and asked me where I'd been.

'Just talking to someone,' I said and knelt on the dusty earth, digging into it with my hands.

That night I couldn't sleep, thinking what reason I could give Kwanza. Should I say that Bishara had stolen something? Or that she'd said bad things about Momma? Or been with a boy? Or should I tell the truth: that my best friend wouldn't play with me any more because her Papa had told her she couldn't? When he came home from the white man's mine he bought two cows, and he said people with cows shouldn't talk to poor people. And he'd bought shoes for Bishara, with brown leather straps and black rubber underneath. She was the only girl in our village who had shoes. And her brother Akili couldn't talk to me, either. Bishara looked sad when she told me – we'd always played together and worked in the fields together but she couldn't now. I looked down at the ground – at those shoes – and she said one day her family would go to live in the town

Cursed

with her Papa, because there was a school there. We'd always talked about what we would do when we were older – about boys and having babies, and how Bishara's Papa always wanted her and Akili to go to school.

What Bishara said hurt nearly as much as when my Papa didn't come back from the white man's mine and Momma said he wouldn't ever come back. The last time he came home he brought me a silver bracelet and said he would buy me shoes next time. He told me he walked for six days to get to the mine and worked in the dark under the ground. He didn't tell me that he slept on a hard floor with eighty other men and it was dangerous in the mine, but Momma told me this when he was away.

'Why does he go, then?' I asked.

'To get some money,' she said. 'There's no money here.'

I lay on the rushes, next to little Matumi, who was curled up asleep. I could hear Momma crying across the hut. She cried when Papa didn't come back but I hadn't heard her cry for a long time. What could I tell Kwanza? Should I just tell him the truth – that my friend wouldn't play with me or talk to me any more? The grown-ups said that you could curse somebody who had been bad to you. Kwanza would understand. I think Momma had stopped crying when I went to sleep.

Patches of Light

I had to wash my yellow dress in the stream the next day while I wore my other dress – the pink one. I took Matumi to the fields again, leaving my dress hanging on a bushwillow to dry. I told Matumi to keep digging while I went to see if my dress had dried, but I went to Kwanza's hut.

'Well, Mkweli, do you still want the curse?' he asked.

'Yes,' I said. 'Put it on Bishara because she won't talk to me now that her Papa has two cows.'

I could see Kwanza's yellow teeth when he smiled. 'Is that a good reason for a curse?' he said.

'She was my best friend and I can't play with her now,' I told him and gave him my bracelet.

'Where did you get this?' he asked.

'Papa brought it back from the mine,' I said.

'Your Papa was a good man… and a friend. You keep the bracelet,' he said and held it out to me.

'Aren't you going to set the curse on Bishara?' I asked.

'I'll do what I have to do,' he said. 'What your father would have wanted. Don't worry about it.'

I grabbed my bracelet and ran back to Matumi.

Momma knew I couldn't speak to Bishara and Akili any more. 'It's a good thing you don't see Akili now,' she said. 'Don't want you havin' no babies. We got enough mouths to feed already.'

I twisted the bracelet around my wrist and wondered how long it would take for the curse on

Cursed

Bishara to work. What would happen to her? Would she get sick or go crazy? Would she fall down? I didn't know what happened after a curse.

Some days she walked past me in the village, wearing those shoes. I said 'Hello' to her at first but she walked on as if I wasn't there so I stopped saying 'Hello.' It didn't look as if the curse was working. Was it going to work?

Three weeks later her Papa got too sick to go back to the mine and people said he was lying in his hut, sweating and coughing. Kwanza did his medicine every day but her Papa died. The next week Bishara and her Momma got the fever and lay in their hut, too weak to get up. Was the curse working at last? It wasn't meant to be on her Momma as well. Was she sick because of the curse on Bishara? I saw Kwanza going into their hut but he didn't notice me.

The next day he came to our hut and gave Momma a pair of shoes with brown leather straps and said Bishara wouldn't need them any more. He looked at me and shook his head and walked off. Momma said I could have the shoes but I told her I didn't want them. I didn't want Bishara to die. If I walked around in her shoes it would keep reminding me what I had done to her.

Momma asked me why I lay on the rushes all morning when there was marula fruit to collect. I told her I was upset about Bishara and didn't want anything to eat. I didn't eat anything for days, thinking about Bishara. Would people find out what I'd done? I'd smacked Matumi for running off and I'd worn Momma's silver necklace but I hadn't done anything bad before. I wouldn't see Bishara again, just like Papa. Kwanza's curse must have been too strong. Would people find out and blame me for what happened to Bishara and her family? That was all I could think about.

Yesterday, when I walked to the trees, I was too tired to pick any fruit and just sat there while Matumi picked what she could reach. I came home and lay on the rushes. Today I got very hot and started coughing; I was sweating so much my yellow dress was sticking to me. I couldn't eat and wanted to drink water all the time; my ribs got sore from coughing so much. I was sick like Bishara had been. Momma went to fetch Kwanza and he made me drink green medicine that tasted like grass. He stood there while I swallowed it all even though my mouth was so dry I couldn't talk properly. After he went I coughed up blood – dark red blood – across the front of my yellow dress, so Momma changed it for the pink one. I'm very, very tired and just want to sleep now. When Kwanza comes tomorrow I'll ask him if getting sick like this only happens to people who have been cursed.

ENVELOPES

Heather Freckleton

The morning is dark. Clouds swoop low over our terraced streets, their black hearts full of rain. It is early and the front doors of houses are like tightly shut mouths. I want to get out and back here before people start leaving for work. I don't want to be seen.

I put on my trainers and take down my duffel coat from the peg making sure the card is still in the pocket. I step out on to the street careful to avoid a Foster's lager can on the doorstep, though I might kick it when I get back, kick it right up against next-door. That'll serve him right, monkey man. He's recently moved in and I saw him washing his car the other day. Stripped to the waist he was and smothered in curly black hair, back and front.

'What are you staring at, goggle eyes, bet you'd like to sink your comb in this lot?' he'd said when he saw me looking. I'd only poked my head out to see if it was raining but I'd kept Dad's reading glasses on.

'You must be joking, monkey man.' And I'd gone back inside. Dad's away for a couple of days visiting his brother in Newcastle and he'd left me a list of things to do. His writing is so bad it took me half an hour to decode even with the help of magnification. Ever since then, monkey man leers and waves whenever he sees me, but all I can think of is his built-in gorilla suit.

Patches of Light

I walk up the road with my hands shoved in my pockets. I can feel the card in its bright red envelope, warm and friendly. Lee's name is on the front and I run a finger over the shape of it. I imagine touching his skin like this, gently. This is the first valentine card I've ever sent but I know Lee is special and soon, he's going to know it too.

I often see him at the jobcentre. He likes to tease me but in a nice way. He says things like, 'You look tired, been up all night with your boyfriend again?' Even though he probably knows I don't have one. He calls me Kaz instead of Katherine or Katy. No-one else does that. His lips are big and fleshy like a satin sofa and he's got a tattoo of a coiled snake all up his left arm. When he looks at me I feel funny like when you look at water on a sunny day and it's full of moving diamonds. I know he's about my age because we were in the same year at school, though never in the same class. He was ugly then; a stick insect covered in spots, always with a gang of mates throwing each other into hedges on the way to school. I hated him at the time and all the other lads looking at us girls with their Alsatian eyes.

Lee lives with his mum. His girlfriend used to live there too, but he told me he dumped her months ago. Amy Cruikshank. Makes me laugh when I remember what we called her at school. I bet he's glad to be rid of her.

In the card I've put, 'To Lee, all my love, Kaz.' It's a brilliant card with two tortoises on the front,

Envelopes

one saying to the other, 'Come out of your shell, Valentine,' then inside, 'or I'll have to come into yours.' It's hysterical, he'll love it.

Lee's lucky to live with his mum even though she's like one of the undead with her streaked hair and concertina face. But he's lucky to have a mum. Mine disappeared to Luton with a lorry driver when I was five. I can remember her a bit; smelled nice, laughed a lot and always kissed me goodnight saying she loved me. She couldn't have meant it though, or she wouldn't have gone off like that, would she? Dad has said she's never tried to contact me but when I think back, I remember him scrunching up unopened post sometimes and plunging it into his pockets. I never found any thrown-away envelopes in any of our bins and I knew better than to question Dad.

I'm nearly at Lee's now. He only lives ten minutes away up Connaught Street. I'm at the corner about to cross over when his front door opens and out she steps; old manky-pants, Amy Cruikshank. There's a trapped bat beating in my head and my mouth is as dry as an old sock. Now there's Lee in his underpants on the doorstep kissing her.

'Laters babe, see you after work.' Then he's gone. And off she struts, thin as a blade up the road towards the bus. I rip up Lee's card, still in the envelope and thrust it into a nearby bin.

No-one has seen me and I'm back at my own front door. The bat in my head has quietened, but I

Patches of Light

can feel the tears pricking the corners of my eyes. Stupid Lee and his rubbish tattoo. Who wants him anyway? He deserves old manky-pants. I don't care, I just don't care. But I know I probably do.

The lager can's gone off the doorstep. As I let myself in, I tread on a square blue envelope on the mat. My name is on the front; just Katy, no surname, address or stamp. At first I think it's from Lee but that's mad, I've just seen him still in his jockeys. Then I think it must be from Mum. She wants to tell me she's loved me all these years and wants to be back in my life and she's sorry, really sorry for leaving like she did. I tear open the envelope. On the front of the card is a raggedy grey bear with a banner saying, 'Will you be my valentine?' Inside are two bears hugging each other surrounded by tiny floating hearts. It's not from Mum. The message is, 'To Katy from Kev.' Then in brackets, 'Fancy a pint later? Will come round about seven.'

Kev, who the hell is Kev? Surely no-one's called Kevin these days? I try and think what else Kev might be short for. Then I remember where I've seen that name recently; when one of monkey man's letters was accidently posted here a couple of weeks ago. Yes, his name is Kevin J. Dawson. I remember because it sat on the table all day before I bothered to put it through his letterbox. But why is Kev the monkey man sending me a valentine? And how does he know my name? I bet Dad told him. I've seen them chatting on their way out to work in the

Envelopes

morning. In my mind I see a gorilla thundering through the jungle, trailing his hands along the ground and flashing his red backside. Only he has Kev's face. I laugh and laugh. I lay the card face down on the table next to its blue envelope. But I am annoyed that he thinks I might be available to go for a drink on Valentine's Day. Even though I am.

I stand at the window and look out at the houses leaning like grey old men. Next time I go to the jobcentre I'll ignore Lee, but I know how easily he can make me laugh. Maybe I'll ask him about Amy just to test him. See if he's still lying. And what shall I say to monkey man tonight? I could just turn off the lights and pretend I'm not in. I've got all day to decide.

It is still early. Broken hearted clouds spill their rain on to shining rooftops. Above the clouds the sky is lightening and I see the postman in his high vis jacket, hair flattened and dripping, coming up our path. The letterbox clatters. Among the usual boring brown envelopes for Dad and a couple of takeaway menus is a large lavender envelope for me. Ms K Simmonds it says in neat writing I don't recognise. The postmark is blurred by rainwater. I take the card into the kitchen. I'm starving. I must get my breakfast before I open it.

HALLQUEEN

Roy Gray

Jeff left the Metropole Hotel late, weaving through a group of tobacco addicts at the doorway, into the throng on the busy Brighton seafront road. A cold wind whipped the smoke away too quickly to register, but it was blowing in his direction, and it was only a mile to Rock Gardens and his hotel so he zipped up his jacket and went with it.

He merged into the pedestrian crowd of youngsters sporting charcoal-blackened eyes, faces and limbs festooned with fibre tip pen stitching and bruises and/or red lipstick wounds. Two in the morning still counted as Halloween, it seemed. Jeff recognised zombies, vampires, bloodstained paramedics, ghosts and a range of movie monsters, though the latter were often guesses, as he certainly could not always identify monster or movie. Most of the girls wore revealing outfits, often artfully tattered, low-cut and/or gaping costumes with short skirts. They made no concessions to the season, apart from a green-stained witch keeping a good grip on her hat. The boys wore similarly decorated short-sleeve summer shirts and jeans, and so had more cover in most instances.

A few vapes glowed among the walkers and amidst clusters of real smokers sheltering in doorways. The traffic included lots of taxis with the

Hallqueen

odd police car and paramedic. No sirens though, no flashing blue lights. Jeff considered crossing the road to see what was happening on the promenade and beach. A barrier of red brake lights, along with the wind being much worse by the beach, decided him against that; his jacket was lightweight, meant for warmer seasons. At least its colouring would make him more visible on dark roads. There were no teen zombies and vampires in view on the seafront side; they preferred the more sheltered side out of the worst of the wind. Some in the crowd were staggering drunk, but others had assumed zombie gaits for selfies with friends' smart phones and cameras.

He passed the queue for the club at the Brighton Centre. Despite the brisk November night, their outfits reflected the Halloween theme and were very unseasonable.

Next the smell of hot fish and chips from youngsters in the street signalled the first of the chip shops on his route and there it was: all steel counter, bright lights, glass front and a queue of scarred zombies – one with a fake axe seemingly buried in his head, bloody nurses, a werewolf and other apparently walking wounded flowing out of the door.

Two a.m.! Jeff took out his iPhone and snapped a picture for Twitter. He checked it. Glare from the window, so he moved round and took another through the open door. Better, so he moved on, phone in hand whilst he tweeted it. The aroma of vinegar and chips on the wind stayed with him, strengthening occasionally as he passed couples and groups sharing, or at least lingering, over their vinegar-flavoured fry ups. Hashtag '#Halloween 2 am! The chip shop queue of nightmares but not dreaming!' he tweeted.

Damn! '#Hallqueen' a bloody typo. He noticed too late. *I'm not correcting it now.*

One shop doorway was shared by an apparently homeless man and dog, but with so many wearing costumes Jeff wasn't absolutely sure. Another contained a couple who had overindulged in food or alcohol or both – the male was lying down with his legs and feet protruding from the recess. A girl dressed as a seeming blood-spattered nurse was squatting next to him holding his head up. People were stepping over the legs, but Jeff stopped. He was a first aider at work so he knew some basics. No bleeding apparent, only fake stains.

'Can I help?' he said. He held up his phone. 'I know some first aid or I can call for help.'

The girl looked up. 'He's had too much to drink but he'll be okay. I am really a nurse. His dad is on the way.' She showed Jeff a phone that had been out of sight behind her patient.

'Okay,' Jeff said, 'Best of luck.'

At the Queens Hotel Jeff forked left out of the crowd through the alley towards Steine Gardens. To his right, he glimpsed a moving shadow and someone rushed out of a dark doorway to grab his iPhone. Jeff staggered and was spun round with his phone as his assailant tried to wrench it away. In reaction, Jeff fisted his left hand and rammed it into the thief's hood. He heard a gasp, then sensed another threat and flinched, but not soon enough. Something heavy and solid slammed hard down on to the side of his head, then on to his right shoulder and somehow bounced back to hit his jaw, or maybe the other way round. There was a second mugger and Jeff's phone was gone in a blaze of pain; lightning shooting down his arm, his jaw throbbing, his head thumping. The first mugger had his phone but couldn't match his partner's pace as they ran back towards the seafront. He's slower from my punch, Jeff decided. So, despite a now unusable right arm, a swelling eye, an extremely sore tongue, a strong taste of blood and something trickling down his face, he ran after him. Back on the front, Jeff caught up and snatched at the phone with his good arm. The mugger spun round and punched Jeff in his stomach.

Jeff fell back and then tried running on, but the pain in his abdomen was unbearable and he looked down to see a handle sticking out of his coat. Stabbed! He knew enough first aid to realise his guts were punctured and, aside from potential sepsis, he'd be bleeding internally. Not a good idea to remove it immediately either, he thought. 'Shit!' wasn't the word for the predicament.

Patches of Light

Suddenly exhausted he lurched across the pavement to slump against a wall. No phone to call. He tried shouting to the passing crowd but all he produced were incoherent croaks. He couldn't speak. His tongue was badly bitten and his jaw must be broken. He could taste lots of blood and feel it trickling from his scalp and mouth. He must look terrible.

He tried to shout again and a young couple, werewolf and vampire possibly, came over.

'That's good,' the werewolf said and took a photo with a flash of his mobile.

Another couple, ghosts maybe, joined them. One of the ghosts came right to the wall, leaning in close enough for Jeff to feel his costume's cowl brush against his hair and recognise tobacco on his breath, as he held his phone out – screen facing away – and flashed a selfie.

Jeff attempted to shout 'Help!', and produced another croak. The vampire replaced the ghost. Then he felt a gentle draught and almost tasted her alcoholic breath. Next her lips, or fang, touched his cheek as her phone flashed in his face. He tried to push her away and felt something soft. She backed away, squealing and laughing.

'This one's a bit of a perv.'

'Thrill of the year for him, doll.' Followed by laughter, mainly male.

Jeff attempted to lunge away but he couldn't move his legs, and when he tried to lean forward his

Hallqueen

coat was caught on something behind him. He wasn't sure if that was good or bad; he could easily fall on the knife or screwdriver.

Amid the sounds – passing traffic, laughing, clicking of digitised shutters – someone said, 'Let me take one.'

Then the vampire's lycan friend called, 'Hold it, doll,' and another flash. Others had seen them and a party of witches, ghouls and devils crowded round laughing, giggling and chatting with mobiles flaring for more photos.

Jeff shivered. *Is there extra bite in the wind?* 'hashtag … Fuck! Typo? Hallqueen?' he heard. *I'm getting weaker, I'm going to faint.* He closed his eyes … 'I'll tweet this now.' More sounds of digitised shutters … 'Let me in' … 'Loads of likes and shares. That was quick' … Hellish red flashes shining through his eyelids … *Surely I'm dreaming, in a nightmare …*
… Maybe
    I
         really
                am …

WEEDING

Robert Angus

Well, I better get on, he thought as he took hold of the armrests and struggled to his feet. That's the trouble with weeding the path – no sooner than you finish and you have to start again. It's like painting the Forth Rail Bridge. He stopped beside the plastic bucket he used to collect the weeds and pushed his foam mat into place with a foot. Each time he knelt down he wondered if he would be able to get up again. What on earth was he doing? He didn't like gardening, but his wife had decided that in addition to mowing the lawn he could tend the path, so what could he do? The gravel hurt his knees and leaning forwards on hands and knees hurt his back but everywhere he looked weeds were appearing between the gravel chips. He could have sworn this area was clear yesterday. New weeds seemed to pop up overnight. Or were they flowers? What really is the difference? Is a flower a weed if it grows in a gravel path? And why is a weed a weed if it's beautiful, and some flowers are ugly?

He shook his head as he reached out for a fine green shoot just appearing between the gravel chips. He was wearing an old pair of leather gloves so he didn't hurt his fingers. It allowed him to sieve through the gravel to get at the roots. Sometimes the root came up easily. Large weeds would come away

Weeding

in his hand with little resistance. Sometimes the tiniest shoot would have deep roots and would cling to the earth and life till he would give up the battle, breaking the stem, then pushing gravel over the remnant in the hope that it would wither from lack of sunlight. Weeds were like people. Some would give up life with hardly a struggle whilst others would fight relentlessly no matter how severe their illness, clinging to life with every fibre of their being. And you couldn't always tell by appearances, with weeds or people. A frail old spinster might put up an almighty fight. And a hulking old bruiser – no sooner had the doctor mentioned cancer than he retreated into himself, dying in a matter of weeks.

    He stopped for a moment and turned to look at the rest of the garden. The lawn was neat as ever. Well, he had cut it only yesterday before starting on the path again. The borders were overgrown. They were his wife's province but she didn't take much care of them any more. She would be indoors drinking tea and eating biscuits while she watched daytime TV. He could see the open back door from where he was kneeling. The front door was locked so she couldn't try to go out without him seeing. But the key wasn't in the lock. The district nurse might come by and she had a key of her own. He wouldn't want to have to get up to let her in, and anyway, he wouldn't hear the front doorbell from here. He separated the gravel chips to get at a stem and pulled at another weed. It came out easily, but the root was

Patches of Light

long and slender lifting a line of gravel as it rose to the surface. Weeds really are like people he mused again, some hard and resilient, some soft and easily dealt with and some with unexpected hidden depths.

    Again he cast a glance at the back door but there was no sign of movement. He had taken his wife out yesterday, just to the local shops, to the supermarket. He had bought her lunch but that was a mistake. No sooner had they taken their seats than he had needed the toilet and at his age his bladder couldn't be ignored. Stay there, he insisted, and eat your lunch, I'll be back in a minute. But it wasn't a minute. His bladder told him to go but his prostate wasn't having any of it. For an eternity he stood at the urinal, urging his bladder to work till at last he felt it dribble, slowly, on and on, and oh the relief at last. He couldn't remember the last time his bladder had let him have a good night's sleep. What a way to grow old, at the mercy of your bladder and your bowels. And when he got back to the supermarket café, she was gone. Her food was there, and his, both plates untouched and her coat was still over the back of the chair, but where was she? He looked round but she wasn't in sight. He asked a man at the entrance if he had seen her, but he hadn't, or hadn't noticed. People don't these days, or don't care. He hurried back in and found her at the breakfast cereals. She was looking at the frosted flakes. She said she liked the blue box. Would she go with him? Well, she might,

Weeding

but who was he? He took her back to their food, but it was cold now and she wouldn't eat it so he ate his lunch slowly while she watched people go by. As always, she spoke her mind, not caring if people heard. 'She's fat, he looks dirty, fancy buying that, what must they be thinking?' He cowered over his lunch hoping no one would take offence and start an argument, then he took her home.

And today was another day, washing done, house tidy, now back to the weeding. He pushed the bucket forward, then moved his foam mat and gently eased himself on to it. Another few feet clear though the bucket was now nearly full. Ivy was beginning to grow on to the path from the border. He cut it with a pair of shears and threw it into the bin. Then forward again, the same old ritual, push the bucket, move the foam mat and carefully ease yourself into a new position. Again on hands and knees he would reach out for any new shoots trying to reach the sun. At last he put both hands on the bucket, pressed hard and tried to stand. It was a slow process taken in steps to protect his knees. When he stood, he could see the district nurse standing by the open back door. She waved.

'I'll be done in a minute,' he called. 'Just a few more feet of path and I'll call it a day.' He pushed the bucket forward, almost to the end of the path where the weeds were well established. He thought these were the sort that you could pull up quite easily, large leaves but little root, but you never could tell.

Patches of Light

He thought his wife would be like them but she had surprised him. She hadn't said anything sensible in years, he did everything for her, and yet when he placed the pillow over her face she had put up quite a fight. He had taken her a cup of tea in bed as usual, but she had still been half-asleep. When she struggled, she knocked the cup of tea over, burning the back of his hand. It took far longer than he had expected. She was like one of those weeds that cling to life, but he had succeeded in the end. What else could he do? She had always told him to get rid of weeds.

'I'll be with you in a minute,' he called again to the district nurse. She was talking to two policemen. She looked embarrassed.

I'D LIKE TO SETTLE DOWN BUT THEY WON'T LET ME

Ian Pickering

Hansen kept to the shadows as he made his way down the sunlit street. The small market town to which the leisurely branch line train had brought him seemed reassuringly unconcerned by his arrival. He gave a swift glance at his reflection in a charity shop window. The five-day-old stubble on his face had yet to reach the stage where it could be called a disguise. Hansen wondered if it would be allowed to.

Just beyond the shop was a pub. Hansen glanced at his watch. Just after 3 p.m. A quiet time. He thought he'd chance it and went in. Inside it seemed comfortingly desolate. The young barmaid who came out of the back room to serve him smiled as he gave his order. There was no recognition in her face. 'I think we are quiet today,' she said in a foreign accent as she gave him his pint of lager. Hansen wondered vaguely which country she came from, but any extended conversation could be fatal so he merely smiled in agreement and moved to a table. When he sat down, he noticed that it wasn't as quiet as he would have liked. As his eyes adjusted he saw that there were two other customers sitting at adjacent tables on the other side of the room.

Patches of Light

Lauren Nicholson gently rotated the glass in her hand as though she were nursing a fine cognac rather than a cheapish gin and tonic. Having illicit time off work always felt luxurious. Nothing beats a fictional dentist's appointment on a boring Tuesday afternoon. No need to fear discovery either. The King's Head in Brantham at just after 3 o'clock on a Tuesday afternoon was not a place to go if you craved human contact. She was therefore unsurprised to find the place empty when she arrived. Since then however, two people had entered the pub. First, there was the strange middle-aged man who had annoyed her by choosing to sit on the next table when he had every seat in the place to choose from. He hadn't attempted to chat her up however, but had immersed himself in a newspaper, surfacing occasionally to visit the bar. He seemed to be working his way along the beer pumps, choosing a different drink each time. She decided he was either an undercover inspector for the *Good Beer Guide* or a very methodical alcoholic. The man who had just arrived interested her more. Probably just the other side of thirty, he was attractively stubbled and tousled. The travelling bag he'd placed on the table made it hard to see him properly and added to his allure. Obviously not a local. Lauren drained her glass. No harm in sashaying past him on her way to the bar. Not that she was too sure what sashaying involved. If it meant walking like you'd just had three gin and tonics and were heading for a fourth then she had it covered, but otherwise not.

Perhaps coincidentally, the man unzipped the travelling bag, looked down and started delving inside as Lauren walked past. Never mind. Get him on the way back.

'You need another?' said the barmaid.

'No, I don't *need* another. I want one,' replied Lauren. It made her sound patronising but the way the girl had asked the question made Lauren think more of a government health advisor than a barmaid. She tried to make amends by smiling as she took the drink but the smile wasn't returned. Ah well. Dim little creature. Now, back to business. Turn around. Sashay, sashay, sashay…

Hansen furtively appraised his fellow drinkers. On the left hand table was an owlish middle-aged man and on the right a slightly blowsy blonde woman of around thirty. It looked like a blind date between George Smiley and Bridget Jones. On closer inspection however, Hansen could see that the pair were not a couple. For one thing, the man was engrossed in either a sudoku puzzle or a crossword and for another the woman was giving Hansen the eye. It was worrying that the man had a newspaper. It was even more worrying that the woman was showing interest in him. She couldn't have recognised him or it would have been over by now but the less time she had to mull over him the better. Best just check the equipment, drink up and go.

As luck would have it, he unzipped the bag and peered inside just as the woman lurched upright and moved toward the bar, passing uncomfortably close to him. A tart remark made by the woman to the barmaid enabled him to check the sound level. Hansen kept his head down and looked up only as the woman retreated to her chair. Did she always walk with that constipated waddle? Time to move on. He raised his glass just as the middle-aged man's wristwatch alarm went off.

Francis Hill had had a satisfactory day so far. After a breakfast of boiled eggs – it was Tuesday – there was the usual anxious wait for the post. When the postman eventually came, he delivered three items of mail. A *Three* day. That meant a train journey of three stops which brought him to Brantham. The Third nearest pub to the station was The King's Head. He walked in and ordered a pint from the third pump along from the left. The first problem of the day then manifested itself. The third table from the window on the left was empty but the second was occupied by a young woman. If he took the correct seat it might look as if he was after her company. It had to be done though. He took a deep breath and walked over, taking care to avoid eye contact, sat down and immediately busied himself with the newspaper. That hurdle negotiated, he composed himself. First drink for the crossword, second for the sudoku, third for the trivia quiz, moving along the pumps each time. The arrival of a third customer who took a seat across the room added a pleasing congruence. This was shaping up to be a perfect *Three* day.

Perhaps he shouldn't have been surprised that it was the woman's fourth drink that broke the spell. Flouncing back across the room she seemed piqued at something and dropped back into her seat with an air of petulance. At that moment his watch alarm started bleeping. It was 3.33. Time to turn to page 3 of the newspaper and place it face up on the table. He did this while disabling the alarm. The theatricality of his actions drew the attention of the woman at the next table and they both looked down at the paper. The upturned page featured a photograph of a man under a headline mentioning a large sum of money. They looked at Hansen. They looked at each other. They moved simultaneously.

Hansen knew he should react but there was something transfixing about the scene. George Smiley and Bridget Jones seemed locked together in a cross between a wrestler's grapple and a lover's embrace. Jones ended this by bringing her knee into Smiley's body, sending him doubled to the floor. She then turned and ran two steps towards Hansen before the heel on her shoe snapped and she sprawled on the floor clutching her ankle. Hansen had almost reluctantly just started to move when a hand dropped on his shoulder and a voice sounded in his ear: 'I think I am knowing you.'

From the *Brantham Gazette* 14th October 2014:

> The King's Head in Station Road was the scene of amazing drama on Tuesday afternoon as Polish barmaid Irena Kalabinska became the winner of the top-rating TV reality show, 'Wanted Man'. 22-year-old Irena correctly identified and apprehended jobbing actor Neil Hansen who for the past five days had successfully evaded detection by the public despite his picture appearing regularly in newspaper and TV adverts. Irena's reward is a cheque for £100,000. This will enable the Krakow University physics graduate, who has been working at the King's Head while on an extended vacation in the UK, to take up an offer of a research fellowship at Harvard. The hidden video camera in Hansen's bag also captured a fracas between two drinkers in the popular town centre pub. The fractious couple, who apparently recognised Hansen just too late, were named as Francis Hill and Lauren Nicholson. The pair were later released from Brantham Infirmary after treatment for a groin injury and a sprained ankle respectively. Mr Hill is a Borrington man who is known to have been barred from many local premises, while Miss Nicholson is thought to work for local engineering firm Higginson Brothers, although last night the company refused to confirm this. Speaking to the *Gazette* last night, Irena said 'I don't need this money, but I think I want it.'

MAKING AMENDS TO A FALLEN ANGEL

Lynne Voyce

'That's Lucifer, the fallen angel,' mother says. 'Once, he was God's messenger.'

'What do you mean, fallen?' asks Abijah as he looks up at the huge, winged man.

'He fell from heaven, cast out for wickedness: a bad angel.'

The bronze sculpture glowers down at the boy, its eyes merely holes, malign determination fixed on its face. Its frozen hair hangs in gleaming auburn waves, falling on polished, muscular shoulders. Abijah thinks the wings look so strong they will lift it off the plinth, so it can swoop around the dome of the art gallery's circular hall, firing lightning bolts at the silent spectators. This is art, just as Abijah had imagined it: awe-inspiring. He touches the metal foot, firm against the bronze base.

'Let's go to the gift shop,' Mother says, tugging at his hand.

He follows her obediently, but just at the gift shop door, turns back to look at Lucifer. Is it possible? He is sure he can see a subtle relaxing in one of the bronze feet, a slight sinking of one of the shoulders, as if the angel is about to walk, maybe even follow him. For a moment he cannot breathe – he is a God-fearing boy and a wicked angel is the stuff of his nightmares. But the thought is quickly

Patches of Light

dissipated by the sudden yank of his arm as his mother drags him through the door.

Soon Abijah has forgotten the Satan. He is consumed by the material delights of the gift shop. Amongst the shining nik-naks and postcards is a pen just like the one Reverend Webster has in his top pocket when he delivers his Sunday sermons. It is a shining blue treasure with a silver clip and nib.

'I want this,' Abijah demands.

'That's far too expensive. Anyway, you'd lose it within a day; a pen like that is meant for adults.'

The sapphire barrel shines so bright it almost hypnotises him. He pictures himself in his little grey blazer, the pen peeking out of his top pocket, looking just like the Reverend, pious and authoritative. 'Please, Mummy.'

'No.' She walks away.

There is no one around. The assistant is busy at the till putting a flaming red, silk scarf in a grey plastic bag. Abijah takes the pen in his hand, puts his arm straight and with his index finger pushes it up his sleeve. The quick, easy movement seems to take minutes on end. His hammering heart becomes audible as a wave of nausea washes over him. But the deed is done. Then, with stiff legs, he walks out of the gift shop to wait for his mum in the circular hall. Again, he feels the pupil-less eyes upon him. Looking up he meets the fiery gaze of the bronze Lucifer. 'Thief,' the statue mouths, 'you are a thief.'

Making Amends to a Fallen Angel

A shock of fear jolts his body, but again he is saved by his mother. 'Oh heavens, Abijah,' she exclaims, grabbing his shoulder, 'I thought I'd lost you.' She marches him across the Minton tiles towards the exit but Abijah can still feel the burning glare of the statue's eyes on his back.

The next morning, however, when Abijah wakes from the soft slumber of the devout, his first thought is of the pen, not of Lucifer. He reaches under his pillow but his contraband has gone. He runs his hand across the sheet and between the folds of the duvet. Had mother discovered it when she came to kiss him goodnight? Or had someone – or something – else taken it? Then he remembers the fallen angel. Are there pupil-less eyes watching? Can he hear the distant beat of bronze wings?

Then Abijah sees the pen on the floor, gleaming against the pale, scrubbed floorboards. Relieved, he leaves his bed and picks it up; it is cold against his fingers. Going to the window, he pushes aside the net curtains, to look at it even more closely in the bright light. But when he parts the nets and glances out he is met by the most disturbing, extraordinary sight he has ever witnessed.

On the pavement below, just in front of the tiny front garden and red brick wall, is a man lying down. He is completely in profile, his arms and legs tucked in, the way Abijah sleeps; the way he has slept since he was a baby. The man wears beige trousers, trainers and a navy blue fleece. At first Abijah wonders if the man was just tired and lay down there in the night, but there is something odd about him. Then he realises what is so strange: the man is flat. There is barely any depth to him. And all around him is a dark liquid, in a splat. It is clear he has fallen: straight from the sky like Lucifer. Abijah rubs his eyes, looks again. Fanning out from the figure are wings, or what look like wings. The concrete of the pavement is cracked, hundreds of tiny little fractures and ripples forming the shape of two wings, one from the figure's back, one from underneath him, as if it is sprouting from the other side of his back. The cracks spread out in the blue grey concrete like the sea through veiny wings of a dragon fly. Abijah knows this is a fallen angel, God's messenger, and the crooked mouth he can see in profile whispers: 'Thief, you are a thief.'

    Suddenly people start to gather around the figure: men in yellow ambulance jackets; Mrs Friskett from next door; police officers. They work on the body for what seems like hours until the carcass is lifted from the pavement and put on a stretcher. Left behind is a perfect imprint: a figure curled up on its side with wings growing out of it. But this mould of a body is not bronze, it is awash with the black-red liquid that Abijah realises now is blood.

It is the next evening, after school. Abijah sits at the window, his legs pressed to the cool plaster wall beneath it. A sheet of paper is on the sill, kept in place

Making Amends to a Fallen Angel

by his forearm. The window and nets are open. It has been a broiling hot day, so much so his head aches from being out in the sun. Beneath him, where the man had lain, is a smooth pool of wet concrete. The workmen must have been when he was at school. They must have hammered and drilled out the imprint of the angel.

Abijah begins to write with his stolen pen. *'Dear God ...'* he begins.

Downstairs in the kitchen, mother prepares dinner while the radio is on. It is barely audible in the bedroom and Abijah is too busy composing his letter to listen anyway. The news says: 'Police concluded the man, found on the pavement of a suburban street, had stowed away in the landing gear of a passenger jet. When the plane lowered this gear, as it neared the runway, the man – probably already dead – had fallen to the ground.' The words float out into the late summer afternoon through the open window, past the patch of wet concrete where the stowaway landed.

Upstairs, Abijah continues his letter. *'I have heeded your warning. I confess, I am a thief.'* The plummy summer scent that warns of a storm circulates around the house. He looks up at the sky: the clouds are gathering low and heavy. The workmen have left the pavement uncovered; he imagines the drip drop of rain on the unset concrete and what it will do. In the distance he hears the growl of thunder. *'I am sorry I stole. I know not stealing is one*

Patches of Light

of the Ten Commandments because Miss Michael at Sunday School has done the five easy ones with us.' Whatever Abijah writes, he knows it won't be as spectacular as the message God sent him: a real life fallen angel. *'I will only use the pen to write good and kind things. I will make amends for my terrible crime for the rest of my life.'* As God is all-seeing and all-knowing, he can read the letter now but Abijah will post it anyway. He'll get a pack of envelopes and a stamp from the corner shop, then address the letter to 'God'. Of course, as God is all powerful, he'll bend the post to his will and the letter will reach him.

Abijah slips on his waterproof coat and creeps downstairs. He knows for sure that Mother would not approve of him going to the shop by himself. He will take the money she gave him for being awarded 'Pupil of the Week'.

Outside, the warm wind is getting blustery. Abijah goes out of the gate and skirts along the edge of the perfect pool of concrete. The privet that edges the top of the red brick garden wall scratches his face. But just in the moment when he passes the perfect waters of the wet concrete, a simultaneous crack of thunder and flash of lightning surprise him so much he loses his balance and finds his new trainers, with him in them, rooted in the liquid cement. The shock of the noise and fiery light has shaken him so much he begins to cry. As if mirroring his emotions, the heavens open. Huge raindrops begin to fall with the kind of force that would have heralded Noah's flood.

Making Amends to a Fallen Angel

As the rain comes, so does the wind. Its hands grab at Abijah's note to God, rip it from his bitten dirty fingers. He watches the note spiral into the air, light and dry at first, then a sodden little scrap that rides the air currents to a faraway place. Maybe to heaven, Abijah thinks. His tear-streaked, dirty face is washed clean by the raindrops. He is, all at once, angelic. 'I'm sorry,' he howls, 'I'm sorry I stole.'

DARREN WHITTAKER

Barbara Oldham

Darren was desperate. Tomorrow would be his mother's birthday. He hadn't got her a present and stood little chance of acquiring one. His present funds amounted to 76p. Not enough to buy a bunch of past-their-sell-by-date flowers from the garage. Gran had refused to lend him any more money until he paid back the last fiver he'd borrowed.

Part-time jobs were impossible to come by. Besides, his mother had told him to concentrate on his school studies. The paper round had only lasted a couple of months until he was sacked for arriving late too many mornings and posting *The Sun* through number 23 Willow Avenue instead of *The Times*. His friends were as broke as he was. Brad had asked him for a loan to take his girlfriend to the new club on the high street. 'I can't, I'm skint,' was his reply. It wasn't that his mother expected a present but she'd be disappointed. He'd feel he'd let her down once more if he didn't turn up with one.

Wait a minute. He suddenly remembered the flyer he'd picked up from the door the other day: something about tenners being handed out. A search around found it amongst the papers ready for recycling. It was from that Happy Clappy vicar from St Chad's offering ten pound notes to be given out at the church hall … today. Darren shot out of the door.

Darren Whittaker

He'd only just make it in time. The offer was only available until 4 p.m. Less than half an hour to go.

Thinking of chocolates, bath stuff, flowers, as well as a decent card, Darren was certain his problem was solved.

'Hello, you're from round here, aren't you?'

'Yeah.'

'Thought so. And you are?

'Darren, Darren Whitaker. I don't come to …'

'Well, Darren, you know you're always very welcome to join us … any time you feel like coming along.'

'Thanks, but …'

'I know it's not "cool" these days to be attending church.'

'It's not that …'

'Don't worry, Darren. I know why you're here.'

Darren froze. The vicar didn't know it was his mother's birthday the following day. How could he? And there was no way he would know about his need for money. 'It's all right, Darren. I'll give you a ten pound note.' Perhaps the vicar did know something, had somehow guessed from the worried look on his face and his dash into the hall.

'Well, if … thanks.'

'I wouldn't offer it otherwise. Now all I ask is that you spend it wisely, spread a little happiness in an unexpected way.'

Patches of Light

'Yes ...' Darren pocketed the money. That his mother would be happy was a given, but what was this 'use it wisely' and 'in an unexpected way'?

He pulled the crumpled flyer from his combat trouser pocket: USE IT TO HELP SOMEONE OUT, DO A GOOD TURN, MAKE SOMEBODY'S WISH COME TRUE. So it wasn't all to do with lending him ten quid to buy a present for his mother's birthday.

Darren thought for a while. He could buy the presents and the card. The vicar would never know. He could avoid the church and the hall for a week or two, or he could give his mother a box of chocolates, her favourite dark ones, a bunch of flowers and a card. Then borrow some money from her a few days later. He could even walk to college, skip lunch for three days and he'd have saved the money.

'Psst ... hey, Darren, it's me ... Sharon.'

Sharon? Of course, Sharon. That weedy girl with the straggly hair. Always hanging around. On the edge of things. He'd got mates he could rely on. But Sharon? He'd never seen her with anyone in particular. He looked at her again. No make-up, a grubby face with tear stains like tramlines down her cheeks, a thin cardigan pulled round her body and a pair of jeans with holes in them. Not the fashionable rips in the denim worn by the other girls in his class. It was as if she'd dressed herself in a charity shop. She came from a single parent family. Well ditto, but his mother cared and he was never hungry.

Darren Whittaker

'What are you doing here?'
'I'm thinking of getting the bus.'
'Only thinking?'
'Well, depends.'
'On what?'
'Nuffin.'
'You mean you haven't got the bus fare.'
'Yeh. Nah.'
'Where you going?'
'Me gran's. Me mam's out and told me to go to me gran's.'

'Hungry? By the shrug of her shoulders he knew the answer. 'I'll take that as a "yes" then.'

Darren felt in his pocket – first his key, then the ten pound note. Slowly drawing it out, thinking his mother could always wait for her present, he made up his mind and thrust the note towards Sharon. 'Here, take it and get yourself some chips. Go on, before I change my mind.' And he disappeared before one or both of them became embarrassed.

Darren thought it was funny how solving one problem had caused another. Still, he didn't regret giving Sharon the money. The expression on her face was worth a thousand thanks.

The following morning he got up early and before leaving for school took up a tray with tea and toast to his mother. On it he placed a home-made card. After wishing her a happy birthday he felt a lot better and his mother seemed pleased by the gesture.

Patches of Light

Still unable to figure out an alternative means of borrowing money, Darren returned home from college at 3.30. He thought about his mother's face that morning, how she'd seemed touched. Presents didn't always have to be bought. With this in mind, he glanced in the fridge. Nothing much there apart from a few lettuce leaves, one tomato and some cheese. However, his mother liked salad. He could make one without too much trouble, boil an egg and add some cheese, grate it and make it more appetising. The top cupboard had a few tins in it. Darren selected one of salmon. His mother's favourite. Then he took a pizza out of the freezer for himself; easily microwaved. He'd have a little of the salad he was preparing, just to show he was willing. If he had it ready for six o'clock, it would give his mother time to wash and change into something more comfortable. He could even cut a couple of branches of that bush with pretty orange berries. If he put them into a vase, it would make it more like a special occasion.

Darren was surprised by how much he was enjoying putting a meal together. In fact, he had just placed the vase on the table when he heard his mother's key in the door. 'Well, two surprises in one day, it must be my birthday or something.' His mother grinned as she tossed her coat on the nearest armchair.

'I'm sorry, mum, I didn't, I couldn't … well, anyway, happy birthday.'

Darren Whittaker

'Say no more, son. I know exactly what's happened. I've had two phone calls, both congratulating me for having such a caring son. The first from the vicar at St Chad's and the second from the grandmother of Sharon. Anyhow, she wanted to thank you for your kindness to her granddaughter. I nearly told her she must have the wrong person. Darren, I rather think you've got some explaining to do. And, before I forget, the vicar said that he was looking forward to seeing you at church next Sunday.

LOST IN TRANSIT

Dominic Teague

'I can't do that,' says the driver. 'You'll 'ave to wait 'til the next stop now, love. Them's the rules.'

I never imagined the word 'love' could be spoken with such marked dispassion.

'I need to get off *here*,' I say, calmly but insistently. 'I have an appointment. It's important.'

'Sorry, love. Not allowed to drop passengers off between stops. Them's the rules.'

'But I have an appointment. At the hospital.'

The corner of his lip curls.

Does he think this is funny?

I glance over my shoulder, directing my gaze through the rear window of the bus and towards the green hospital roof beyond. It's receding further into the distance with each passing second.

How could you have been so clumsy, missing your stop like that? You know how important this session is. Of course you know; you've lost enough sleep worrying about it.

'Please!' Composure yields to frustration. 'I have an important appointment at the hospital and I need to get off—'

'Look, love, I've told you: I can't pull over until the next stop. Them's the rules. You should've got off at the last stop if you were wantin' the hospital.'

'I tried. You didn't give me a chance!'

'Two other passengers got off in time. I can't arse around all day waitin' for you.'

My grip tightens on the pole, and as it does so I feel Braille dots impressed upon my palm. It's the 'stop' button. I jab it three times in quick succession. The electric 'bus stopping' sign awakens to a triad of chimes.

The driver barely reacts.

I'm about to reissue my appeal, when suddenly he shifts into a lower gear and eases on the brakes. We're slowing.

Not so unreasonable after all.

I move towards the door. The driver shoots me an angry look.

'Stay behind the line, please.'

'I'm getting off now.'

He shakes his head.

Through the windscreen, stretching as far as the eye can see, is a seething column of stationary traffic.

You should've left the house earlier.

How could I possibly have known this would happen?

You should've allowed for the possibility.

I run my hand through my hair in frustration.

Outside it's over 30 degrees. Inside it's a sauna. The humidity's shaded my azure blouse a royal blue, saturating my armpits into sticky oil slicks. I raise my elbows to invite air beneath them, but there is no air to invite. I lick my lips and taste salt.

The other passengers idly fan themselves with copies of *Metro* while pretending not to observe me.

'Can I get off now?' I ask, lowering my voice to a more discreet volume.

The driver sighs. 'I've told you: I'm not allowed.'

'But the bus isn't moving.'

'Doesn't matter. Them's the rules.'

'Why is it a rule?'

'Health and safety.'

'But the bus isn't moving! You could open the door right now and I could literally step out on to the pavement!'

'There's a gap.'

'You call that a gap? Seriously? It's 15 inches tops. I'm not going to get run down by a car in a gap of 15 inches.'

The driver sets his jaw and continues staring at the smouldering chain of metal piled in front of him. It's now become a matter of pride to him; he's not brooking any resistance, and he's not letting me alight until he deems it appropriate.

I consult my watch: nine minutes until the appointment. It'll take me longer than that just to get there.

In desperation, I consider getting myself thrown off the bus. The most appealing violation of commuter protocol would be an assault on the driver, but I don't fancy testing a temperament like his. Not when this tailback's got him riled enough already.

Lost in Transit

Try appealing to his sympathies. Cite your diminished faculties as an excuse for missing your stop.

That seems a more viable option, even though my faculties aren't truly diminished.

Wasn't that the whole point of this session? To determine if those early signs –

Women my age don't get dementia, or Alzheimer's, or other similar such conditions. I'm only 59. And with all the exercise I do, all the dieting and healthy living, I could easily pass for a woman in her forties. I still turn heads when I go to the pool, and I still know a hawk from a handsaw. My mind and body are both up to spec, thank you very much.

Then why are you so afraid of attending this appointment?

I'm not. I just want to get it over with. It's not like I missed my stop on purpose.

The engine gurgles. A vibration shudders through the pole beneath my hand. The bus lurches forward all of four feet. Then issues a frustrated hiss. And stops.

'Oh, for God's sake! At this rate it'll be hours before we crawl to the next stop.'

The driver glares at me. It's the first instance he's deigned to make eye contact this entire time. 'What d'you want me to do about it, aye? Get out and lift the bleedin' bus over the traffic?'

At that moment, another passenger – a young man – rises from his seat and makes his way to the front of the vehicle.

'I'll get off here, thanks, mate.'

The driver grunts and wipes a bead of sweat from his brow. 'I can't let you off 'ere. I have to pull over to the curb to let you off. And I can't do that 'til the next stop.'

'But the bus isn't moving,' says the young man.

'That's what *I* said.'

'We'll be at the next stop soon,' says the driver.

His tone is less hostile when he addresses the young man. Does he dislike me because I'm female? Or is it my accent? Perhaps he resents taking orders from all well-spoken, middle-class commuters, regardless of gender.

And of course you yourself harbour no assumptions or class prejudices related to bus travel.

I'm here, aren't I?

Why didn't you just drive? You could have avoided all this hassle.

I felt like taking the bus. I thought it would be easier.

That's a lie. You didn't drive because you don't trust yourself at the wheel.

A mental image conjures itself before my mind's eye, and I see myself, the week before last, driving to work at 8:30 in the morning. It's a route I've driven hundreds of times. And yet by 8:45 I'm lost. By 9:15 I'm stopping to ask for directions.

How could I have gotten so muddled?

Lost in Transit

Pondering this, the urgency of my appointment reasserts itself. According to my watch, I was due at the hospital three minutes ago.

A child complains somewhere near the back of the bus. Her screeching surmounts the buzz of the engine and stabs at my ears like nails on a chalkboard. The Vauxhall in front farts filthy black smoke against the bus's windscreen. How is it cool air can't penetrate the vehicle's confines, but the stench of exhaust fumes can? It mingles with the smell of sweat and the resultant odour fills my nostrils.

Damn this heat. It's unbearable. I'm finding it hard to breathe.

I have to get off this bus.

Don't wait. Just go. This is important.

Panicking, I lunge at the door and start fumbling with the manual release mechanism.

'Oi! Get away from there!' shouts the driver. He kills the engine and begins disentangling himself from his seatbelt.

The young man backs away, not wishing to get caught in the crossfire. I continue pushing and pulling at the door until it finally yields. I clear the 15-inch gap between the bottom step and the pavement in a single bound.

The air outside hits me like a glass of water. It's still warm, but compared to the furnace within the bus it's a blessed relief.

The driver hurls an obscenity at me from the bottom step.

What's he going to do? Drag you back aboard and keep you prisoner until he reaches the next stop?

No, he realises it's over. He lost. I won. His parting words of abuse are a puerile attempt at levelling the score.

Sighing, I set off in the direction of the hospital. I take a shortcut down a residential walk, following the serpentine curve of the pavement as it winds between the houses.

Before long I reach a junction. And stop.

Which way?

In an instant, my bearings have left me. I can't remember which direction I came from. I select a path and start walking, hoping the sight of something familiar will help reorientate me.

This is absurd. My mind is clear. But I feel as though a thread has snapped somewhere inside my brain. Now I'm struggling to re-establish the connection.

But it can't be anything serious. Things like that don't affect women my age. I'm sure the specialist at the hospital will confirm this.

Just as soon as I get there.

PIG MAN

Margaret Holbrook

It's a quiet day today. Slack for us really. Slack for me.

I knew it was going to be like this today. The Boss said. He told us all yesterday there wouldn't be so many through, not today. Tomorrow and Friday will be slack too, so he says.

Last week was busy. We had to deal with two and a half thousand every day. Two and a half thousand pigs; and not one of 'em over ten months old.

It's not put me off pork though. Bacon, I eat bacon and I enjoy it. I like to dip my bread in the fat as I make a bacon sarnie. I love the sweet taste. I started off young, mind. It's what my granddad did, when he was minding me; when I'd come in from school and was waiting for my mum to pick us up. He was a card my granddad, and he had this ritual, particularly if it was cold. He'd feel my hands first. It used to make me laugh. He'd feel my hands and then say, *'Yes, I think they're cold enough for a butty.'* And that was when the frying-pan would come out.

Gran would have the bacon cut on number eight. That's quite a thick cut. That's when grocers' shops used to cut their own bacon. Slice it from the piece. Now it all seems pre-packed. You've no choice; you get what you're given. Anyway, Granddad would set the bacon frying and while that was cooking he'd slice a good piece of white bread. It had to be white, the bread. It tastes better, that's all. The bread was delivered from the local baker. It was brought to the door in a big wicker basket every Tuesday. Two large, white loaves. That was what made it, you see.

The bread Granddad cut had a crusty top, slightly brown but not burnt, and it tasted, *oh*, how it tasted. And when the bacon was cooked he'd take it out of the pan, set it on a plate and then dip the cut, white bread into the bacon fat. There was nothing like it. I felt like a king. And all the while Granddad was doing this, Grandma would have put the kettle on, brewed up a pot of tea. A bacon butty and a mug of tea, could things get any better?

I never wanted much to eat when Mum got me home. She used to grumble sometimes, but I know it was only put on. She didn't really mean it.

Anyway, my affiliation to bacon didn't end there. It began there. When I left school I became a pig man.

Pig man. It's what my dad and my granddad did. Guess it must be in the blood. Three generations. It's like a tradition; and none of us was put off eating meat. None of us.

My wife's a veggie. Not that I or my job have put her off meat. She was a veggie when we met. I think she wanted to convert someone, me. She didn't manage it.

Pig Man

She can't see how I can do my job, but I tell her, *'It pays the mortgage.'*

Now, cast your mind back a few years if you can. Do you remember the tale of the *Tamworth Two?* They were the Tamworth pigs who escaped their slaughter and lived happily ever after. That's what was in all the papers. They even made a film about it. I've heard that none of it was true. It just made a good story. That's what a mate said, anyway. I don't know, can't vouch for it like, but I suppose it made a good film for the kiddies. And everyone'd like to think they got away, believe that they escaped the pig man, wouldn't they? Even I *want* to believe it.

Like I said, this week'll seem quiet, just two thousand a day through for the rest of the week. It'll seem like a breeze. Roll on weekend.

I don't let it get to me, the killing, and I don't look at their eyes. I can't. I'd not sleep at night if I did, and I need my eight hours. I'm knackered if I don't get enough sleep.

My wife used to say, *'I can't believe you get through so many pigs in a day, every day,'* but I told her, *'When you go shopping, look at all the meat there is on the shelves; cooked ham, bacon, sausage, sausage rolls, pork pies,'* and it goes on, an endless list, really. I said to her, *'It's not there for nothing; it's there because people are eating it.'* She had to agree with me, then. She'd not thought of it like that before. It made her come to earth with a bump. Lives in fairy-tale land sometimes, I think.

And it's not like we're the only place doing this. It's happening all over the country, and in similar numbers. So times our two thousand by however many places slaughter pigs, and, well numbers aren't my strong point, but in a month I've heard it's about, well it's over seven hundred thousand head of pigs slaughtered. And that's just pigs. *Just pigs.*

Can you believe it, the numbers? It's scary, eh? My wife found it difficult to think of the numbers. To think of all those young pigs. She looked at me when I told her all this, looked at me and then said, *'They're only babies. And they're all leaving farms every day. Not knowing they'll never see their friends or the day again.'*

'I know,' I said, *'but they're needed. That's why there's so many pig farmers breeding so many pigs. Without the meat industry there'd be nothing. You wouldn't see them at all, the farm animals. It's the same with sheep. If we didn't eat lamb, they wouldn't exist like they do. There'd be no lambs in the fields at spring-time.'*

She couldn't believe that life wasn't so pretty. It's a good job she married me. I put her straight, or try to.

A CIVILISED MARRIAGE

Tom Kilcourse

I was raised by parents who were mutually intolerant of dissent and constantly embattled. They cared not who witnessed or was embarrassed by their conflict, and appeared to believe that decorum was a place in Italy. Though no punches were thrown they would scream at each other, nose to nose and on the edge of violence. I became sensitive to the early signs, usually a trivial spark, and would absent myself quickly from their presence to take sanctuary in my bedroom. From there I could hear the raised voices, the slamming of doors, and occasional crash of broken glass or crockery. Such was the normality in which I grew up.

When, in my late teens, I met Angie and was introduced to her parents, I was seduced by contrast. The stillness of her home was palpable. Such tranquillity came naturally to Angie, who was raised by mutually taciturn parents. Paul Chesterton, Angie's father, was ever courteous, almost withdrawn, while his wife was barely more voluble. Meals were taken in silence, save for the odd polite request for something to be passed across the table. I felt a little awkward at first in such an atmosphere, though I preferred it to the trenches of my own home, but over the months of our courtship I became accustomed to the Chesterton way of things.

Patches of Light

I spent much time in Angie's house and had the opportunity to study her parents' behaviour. Not once did I hear a voice raised in anger. Disagreement that would have had my parents in noisy confrontation caused only a lifted eyebrow or slight shake of the head. Sometimes, even those signs were absent as one of her parents simply left the room in silence, carefully closing the door behind them. Usually, it was Paul who conceded, with a smile. I studied, and admired him, unconsciously adopting his mannerisms as my own.

I was ill-prepared to see beneath the surface of the Chesterton household. Attracted by their apparent contentment, I adopted behaviours that were alien to me, desperate to show them that I was worthy of their daughter's hand. I believe old man Chesterton was unconvinced, but his wife took to me, and Angie followed her mother's counsel. Our wedding was a restrained affair, nothing flashy, the occasion marred only by a row between my parents.

We bought a house a few miles from the Chesterton home. Naturally, it seemed, we followed the pattern set by Angie's family rather than mine. We never had a row throughout our years together, not once shouting in anger. That sort of behaviour was for other types, those with little self-respect, such as my parents. We took pride in that and, if I'm honest, became a little pompous, looking down on rougher types. Only later did I come to see that such stillness was a sign of deeper, dangerous currents. As

A Civilised Marriage

an older and, hopefully, wiser man I can see that the occasional explosion would have been healthier, an indication that we felt safe enough to quarrel when there was disagreement now and then. Sometimes a raised voice would have been better than a raised eyebrow and silence. Our more 'civilised' behaviour was a sign, not of the superiority we presumed, but of fragility in our relationship. The union promised happiness, but it was a lie.

My parents rarely called to see us, for which I was thankful, but the Chestertons were frequent visitors. Angie's father appeared to embrace me, often saying 'You're family now, Edward', and I believed him. Looking back, I see that he used the phrase to control rather than reassure. If he disapproved of something I said or did he would give a slight smile, and utter those words quietly. It worked. I was in thrall to the apparent sophistication of my unexcitable role model.

It took some time before I began to appreciate that belonging to the family, something I desperately wanted, differed from being a part of it. I think now that my true status equated roughly with that of a family dog. I was tolerated gently and spoken to softly while my views were ignored: not discussed, simply ignored. I noted this pattern, but discounted its importance. Even when, against my expressed wishes, our daughter was christened, I did not create a fuss, accepting Angie's explanation that her mother would be terribly upset if the child was not baptised.

Later, when the two boys were born, I did not even mention my objections.

You may well believe that I am the architect of my own failing, and you would be right, but habit is an insidious trap, and I developed the habit of lying to myself, of believing what I wanted to believe. I valued what I thought others had, dignity, self-restraint and sophistication. I had come to disassociate myself from my own parents' standards.

I claim no excuse for my perceptual myopia: there were many signs over the years that I chose at the time to ignore. Seven years after our marriage, Paul Chesterton died of a heart attack. I recall clearly my surprise at his widow's apparent lack of grief, either before or after the funeral. Not a tear was shed, by her or her two daughters. I chose to interpret that as stoicism, an admirable quality. I know now that it was nothing of the kind. Emotion was not apparent simply because it was not there. Gloria Chesterton and her two girls, Angie and Veronica were, and are, empty of passion or even interest in others.

With her father gone, Angie absented herself from our home with increasing frequency to visit and stay with her widowed mother. She took the children with her. Fear of being thought churlish prevented any expression of protest. Over the following years the nuclear family comprised Angie, Veronica and their mother. They were the centre around which the children, Veronica's and ours revolved. Their development was determined by the

A Civilised Marriage

matriarchy, while my views and those of Veronica's husband counted for nothing.

After a few years of this, Veronica's husband, James Collins, walked out on his wife to live with a woman he had met in his work. I found myself swimming in a sea of vituperative appraisal of his desertion of a 'lovely' wife and mother. People who barely knew him spat out his name, expressing astonishment that any man could so callously break up such a happy home. In cowardice, I remained silent, simply noting that the sole concern of the deserted woman and her mother appeared to be the effect on their image.

A year later, I too had an affair with a colleague. Riven by guilt I eventually told Angie what had happened, fully expecting her to be distraught, though with dignity. She took the news with surprising calm, remaining silent for a minute or two before declaring that she would not interfere, but I must be discreet. I realised then that I would have much preferred to have her respond as my mother would. She would have demanded to know who the woman was, and stormed off to find her. The resulting confrontation might have lacked dignity, but passion would have been evident. It did not please me to know that my wife didn't give a damn what I did, so long as it was done on the quiet.

It was then that I recalled Gloria Chesterton's lack of distress at the loss of her husband, and knew that my wife was cast in the same mould. I decided to leave. I find it interesting to note that, despite their early verbal punch-ups, my own parents are still together, while Angie and Veronica both live only with their children. In my parents' home humour has displaced anger, with each referring to the other with outrageous names, and laughter at the other's foibles. I stay with them frequently.

THE WRITING GAME

David Bryan

'Thank you, Elaine. Your story is very promising. If you leave it with me, I'll jot down a few suggestions regarding structure and dialogue. Incidentally, did you enjoy my collection of poems?'

'I haven't had time to read them. You only gave me the book last night.'

'Did I? Anyway, let's move on. Can we have another volunteer? How about one of the men? I don't want to be accused of bias. Ha! Ha!'

'Can we go for a coffee?'

'Not yet, Chris. We only started twenty minutes ago. Why don't you share your offering with us first?'

'My throat is really dry. I'll be able to read it a lot better after a coffee.'

'I'm sure you can manage without liquid refreshment. Just think of all the struggles the great writers went through on your behalf.'

'But they didn't have dry throats, only cash flow problems.'

'Chris, we are wasting valuable time. Read your story and then, I promise you, we'll go for a coffee.'

'All right. It's called "The Clown". Before commencing, I would like to make it clear that all characters appearing in this work are fictitious. Any resemblance to real persons, living or dead is purely coincidental.'

'Thank you for reassuring us. Now get on with it.'

Once upon a time there was a clown called Charlie. He was a very unhappy clown. Nobody would laugh at him and, to be perfectly honest, years had passed since he last raised so much as a titter. The other clowns had tried to help him but without any success. Poor Charlie was as funny as third degree burns.

'I don't like that bit about third degree burns. It's unnecessary. Furthermore, you haven't told the reader what Charlie looks like.'

'It doesn't matter what he looks like.'

'Yes it does. We need to build up a picture of him in our minds.'

'Why?'

'Because it makes the clown more real to us if we know his physical characteristics.'

'How can he be made more real when everybody knows he is fictitious?'

'A skilful writer is able to do this. So let your creative juices flow and go for it.'

'He was of average height, medium build and had brown hair.'

'Is that it?'

'Sorry, I almost forgot. He had a big red nose.'

The Writing Game

Charlie became so depressed that he decided to leave the circus and get an ordinary job. When he was young he had been good with numbers and his father had told him that one day, if he worked hard, he could become an accountant. Charlie was not impressed and had joined the circus instead. Now he started to think that perhaps it wasn't such a bad idea after all. So he set off towards the centre of the nearest large town. He knew he would find offices there and he also knew that accountants worked in offices.

'What was the weather like when he set off?'
    'I've no idea.'
    'It's your story.'
    'Who cares what the weather was like?'
    'A detailed description of the weather can enhance the mood of the story.'
    'It was pissing down.'

After a while, he met a small boy who asked him why he looked so sad.

'You need to describe the boy in greater detail.'

After a while, he met a very small boy who asked him why he looked so sad. Charlie explained everything and was about to go on his way when a little voice piped up.
    'What's a countant?'
    'You mean accountant.'
    'Yes. What's one of them?'
    'He's a man who sits at a desk all day and does sums.'

'That sounds boring. Does he have any toys?'
'No.'
'Does he play with his friends?'
'No.'
'Is he allowed to watch cartoons?'
'No.'
'Does he make people laugh?'
'I don't know. Maybe if he gets the sums wrong.'
'And you want to leave the circus to become one of those?'
'Yes.'

'I worked in accountancy before I became a writer.'
'So the rumours are true'
'What rumours?'
'You spent twelve months in therapy to get over it.'
'Don't be facetious. Carry on reading.'

The boy stared at the clown in utter amazement. He could not believe his ears. What a silly man. In fact, he was so silly he was funny. Very funny. Tears began to roll down his cheeks as he went into a fit of uncontrollable giggles. At first Charlie did not understand what was happening. Then it struck him like a thunderbolt.
'You're laughing at me!'
'I can't help it. I've never heard of anything so funny. Fancy wanting to be a countant.'
The clown did not bother to correct him again. He was too excited. A plan had come into his head.

The Writing Game

'Did you have a plan in your head when you started writing this?'
'Not really. I like to make it up as I go along.'
'You surprise me.'

Charlie decided to invite his biggest fan to that evening's performance.
'What's your name?'
'Michael.'
'Would you like to come to the circus tonight, Michael?'
'Yes please.'
'Bring all your friends. I'll tell everybody you are coming.'
The clown and the little boy shook hands and said goodbye. Shielding his eyes from the sun –

'I thought it was raining.'
'It was but it stopped. I thought if the sun came out it would mirror Charlie's new optimism. I'm enhancing the mood of the story like you said. Can I continue?'
'Go ahead.'

Shielding his eyes from the sun, Charlie ran back to the circus as fast as he could. He spent the rest of the day trying on different costumes and painting his face. The hours passed slowly but eventually it was time for the show to begin. He took a furtive look inside the big top.

Patches of Light

There was hardly a vacant seat. The music started and the ringmaster made his entrance to tremendous applause.

One by one, the performers went through their routines. Now it was the turn of the clowns. Charlie began to panic. Had he made a mistake coming back? He decided to go and hide somewhere but it was too late. One of the other clowns pushed him into the arena. There was no escape. He looked round frantically for Michael and saw him waving. Ignoring the rest of the audience, Charlie darted over to him and whispered in his ear.

'I want to be an accountant.'

Michael let out a loud guffaw and, because laughter is so infectious, his friends soon joined in. Before long everyone was looking at Charlie and splitting their sides. It was the happiest day of his life.

Charlie quickly became the most popular clown in the circus. He never had any more difficulty in getting people to laugh. He simply went over to the nearest small boy in the crowd and told him exactly how an accountant spent his life.

THE END

'I've written THE END at the end so the reader knows it's the end.'

'Good idea. Always show consideration towards one's readers. Even the possibility of another paragraph could prove fatal for those of a nervous disposition.'

'I presume, by that remark, you don't have a high opinion of my work. I thought it resembled a Maupassant short story.'

'Maupassant?'

'The French bloke who died of the pox.'

'I know who Maupassant is. He would turn in his grave at the comparison.'

'How can he turn in his grave? You can't move when you're dead. And talking of death, I'm going to die of thirst soon.'

'I wonder …'

'You're wondering if you should come to my funeral.'

'No, I wonder …'

'You're wondering if you should have skimmed or semi-skimmed milk with your coffee.'

'No, I wonder …'

'You're wondering if they are still serving toast.'

'No, I wonder …'

'You're wondering if you should have marmalade on your toast, because you have inside information that they have extended their usual toast serving times by twelve and a half minutes.'

'No, Chris. To be perfectly honest, I was wondering if my old firm would have me back.'

FOR YOURSELF ALONE

Cathy Bryant

> *... only God, my dear,*
> *Could love you for yourself alone*
> *And not your yellow hair.*
> W.B. Yeats, 'For Anne Gregory'

Prince Fortin arrived at the tower, dismounted, and stared up at the window.

'Darling,' he called up softly.

Punza heard the call and was half-excited, half-wistful. She had long resigned herself to the imperfections of the tiny world inside her tower, but was finding it a struggle to cope with those on the outside. Illusions (or even delusions) they might be, but thoughts of happiness beyond her prison were all that had kept Punza going during her incarceration.

She sighed and went over to the window, leaned out, and smiled at the Prince.

He was handsome, Fortin, with a tall firm body, clear blue eyes and a sweep of auburn hair; better-looking than I am, thought Punza ruefully. I have only one claim to beauty.

She didn't love him, but would marry him as he had begged, if he rescued her. She had learned not to expect too much.

For Yourself Alone

'Punza, Punzel, Little Rapunzel, Punzelina, Punzerella,' breathed Fortin. 'Let your hair down, darling. It's all I can touch of you.'

Punza nodded, and began to gather up armfuls of the extraordinary mass of tawny-gold. She brushed it and washed it during her time alone, as there was very little else to do; and besides, it smelt and felt terrible when it was dirty. But its gleaming went beyond simple hygiene. It was a spell, and one that could not be broken unless she was rescued from her phallic tower. Still, as curses went, it was a beautiful one – endless, unbreakable corn-yellow hair, filling her cell and keeping her warm on cold nights.

Armful after armful Punza heaved out of the window, and finally found the ends, which tumbled down the full fifty feet of the tower to the ground like rays of liquid sunlight. Fortin grabbed the waves and buried his face in them, kissing them and murmuring things that Punza could not hear. Soon he was enveloped completely in the mass, like an actor who disappears behind a curtain. Punza could hear noises and feel slight tugs, but couldn't see just what he was doing.

She closed her eyes and imagined the touch of another human being. It had been years now. She remembered closeness and warmth, and all the different smells – perfume, fresh sweat, oranges from that nurse of hers who ate three every day. She yearned for both that intimacy and a new kind, something she could not have named but that her body craved.

Fortin emerged, a little dishevelled, breaking her reverie.

'Darling Punza, I have news!' he called. 'I have been given a magic key, and I may unlock your door – but only from the inside of your chamber. To get you out, I have to get in.'

'Oh! Yes – that's wonderful,' said Punza, surprised. 'But my captor will return in less than an hour! We must hurry!'

'The tower is bespelled against ladders, as we know,' said the Prince. 'There's only one way to do it – I'll climb your unbreakable hair! Tie yourself to the bed with it, so that it can support my weight.'

This is a bad dream, decided Punza. I have to tie myself up with the hair he loves? Is this some sort of strange man-woman game? And why didn't he tell me about the key immediately, rather than playing with all that stuff for ages? He is like a wasp around honey; and wasps sting.

But she had no choice if she wanted to escape the tower, which she did. So she wound her hair around the bed and knotted it as best she could, and called to Fortin to climb up.

Well, the bed was the heaviest thing in the room but was still only a spartan single, and Fortin was a tall and hefty young man; and the bed worked its way to the window, and the knots unravelled themselves or broke the bed legs one by one, and Punza screamed.

For the hair might be unbreakable, but her scalp was not, and the higher Fortin climbed, the more hair ripped out of its follicles, which bled. Thick as it was, it pulled out in hanks, leaving bare bloody patches on Punza's head. She would have fallen out of the window almost immediately if she hadn't become jammed between the bed and the lintel, and her head was badly wrenched.

She couldn't help sobbing, and Fortin heard.

'Do not worry, my dove! I'll be with you soon,' he cooed, thinking her frightened, though full ells of bloody-ended hair must have fallen past him by now. There was barely a handful left as he grabbed wildly for the window and pulled himself through, the last locks of hair dropping off as he did so.

For a moment he collapsed on the floor and got his breath. Then he stood up and helped Punza to her feet, and took his first proper look at her.

He saw a plain young woman, quite bald, with red patches on her head like a hood, and her eyes and nose blotched and rimmed from crying. He was startled. This was not what he had expected of his sweet blonde sunshiny damsel.

'The key?' asked Punza softly, seeing his face but desperate to escape the chamber anyway.

'Yes of course, my lady,' replied Fortin, with a formal bow that saddened her.

Patches of Light

But he took a golden key from his tunic and opened the door as simply as that, and they walked down the spiral staircase in silence, all spells broken.

Outside the tower Punza took a lungful of free fresh air, and felt the breeze on her face and all over her body, and wanted to laugh; but Fortin's face was still disappointed, and had a look of the prison about it, she thought.

She freed him.

'Fortin, I am very grateful for your rescue of me,' she said. 'But we need not marry. I don't believe that it is our destiny, and I don't think we'd be happy, either.'

Fortin made to argue, changed his mind, and smiled gratefully.

'As my lady wishes,' he said warmly. 'Is there any other service I can perform for you before I return to my homeland?'

Yes, give me money, food, drink, clothes, a map and your horse, Punza thought, but didn't say. She shook her head and smiled, and headed for the forests she had seen from her prison. They seemed like the best way to evade her captor, albeit dangerous in their own right.

As she reached the treeline she paused and looked back. Fortin was still there, stuffing his saddlebags to bursting point and then every fold of his clothes or inch of his boots with the perfect tresses. From time to time he would kiss them, or wipe his eyes on them, as his shoulders shook. Punza hoped he would leave before her ex-captor returned.

She turned away and headed into the forest, where the green leaves were just starting to turn the most exquisite – even breathtaking – yellow and gold.

FEMALE 198

Annest Gwilym

Mark and Alice drive out of the city into the lush late-summer countryside of Avaldore. They pass field upon field of strawberry and raspberry farms, with tanned and sun-hatted harvesters picking the ripe fruit along the tramlines of the crops.

After the smog and grime of the city, the air here is honeyed, sweet and thick, laden with sun and pollen, buzzing with life. You can almost taste it. They relax for the first time in months. After a couple of hours of driving they see the sign for Genesis.

The Genesis compound runs along to their left for a couple of miles. Its high austere walls are topped with wire fencing, barbed wire and CCTV cameras. It looks more like a prison complex than anything else, and this impression is reinforced when they see the guard tower and armed security personnel standing to attention like soldiers at the entrance.

Genesis has asked them to bring their passports and birth certificates with them, and these are briskly checked by the guards at the entrance, while another guard quickly frisks them and goes over their car. They are given the all clear, and told where they should park.

Female 198

'So, you would like to commission a child from us?' asks Dr Holm, after briefly introducing himself. He is a tall silver-haired man with bright blue eyes and ruddy skin.

Alice confirms that they were both passed as infertile six months ago, showing him the documentation sent to them by the clinic.

'And you have selected the parents you would like from the catalogue?'

Mark replies that they have selected Male 112, and Female 198, and would like to meet them both. They have chosen the male and female who they felt most closely resembled themselves.

Dr Holm explains that during these times of high global infertility levels, Genesis is the world's biggest and most successful baby farm. All their parents have been carefully bred for optimal physical, mental, and intellectual excellence, and reared so that these qualities are maximised with the perfect diet, exercise regime, fresh air and education. They are rigorously checked each month to ensure that the company's high quality standards are being maintained. Mark and Alice silently glance at each other.

To go to the Viewing Room, they follow Dr Holm along a long shining corridor. Unlike the forbidding quasi-military exterior, the inside of the building is expensively, if a little clinically furnished. Pristine white marble walls with grey veining like perfect human flesh, polished to a high sheen, designer furniture in cream leather and gleaming chrome, and fragrant vases full of white lilies on mirrored tables, in huge cut-glass vases.

Instead of the usual bland paintings, large antique bevelled Venetian mirrors have been placed on the walls to reflect back and intensify the light in its silvery glassy brilliance. The effect is of surreal, dream-like and almost overwhelming luminosity.

'This would be a nightmare if I had one of my migraines,' thinks Mark.

He feels as if he has been roughly awakened after the somnolence of the countryside on their drive here, like having to reluctantly get out of a warm bed on a cold and frosty morning.

The Viewing Room is decked like a high-end hotel lounge, and Alice and Mark sit on a cream leather sofa, holding their complimentary cups of aromatic dark coffee.

Male 112 comes in first and sits opposite them, next to the Doctor. He is taller and a bit swarthier than Mark, but otherwise there is a slight resemblance. His voice is rich and low, but there is something a little disconcerting about him, a certain lack of sparkle. Mark can't help but notice his expression of cow-like docility, and thinks to himself: *the lights are **on** ...*

Female 198 is an entirely different proposition. She has a sharp, challenging look about her as she comes to sit with them. Her hair is auburn, long with a natural wave, and she has a foxy shrewdness

Female 198

completely absent in Male 112. A lazy swagger in her walk that says: *don't mess with me*. Her skin is a cool greenish cream often found in redheads, like some elusive underwater creature.

Her left eye is blue-grey and her right eye brown. There is something captivating and dangerous about her, and Mark can't help but stare at her mesmerised. She looks straight at Mark boldly.

'Blue eye – good fairy, brown eye – bad fairy, which are you ...?' he thinks.

Her stance seems to shout: *you have my body, but that's all*. He's never met anyone like her.

'We do not normally tolerate physical imperfections in our parents, but in the case of Female 198, the difference in eye colour is more than compensated for by an extremely high IQ, and besides, some people prefer something a bit different,' assures Dr Holm.

That night Mark's dreams are full of Female 198's vixenish presence. He is waiting for her at the far end of the Genesis complex, by the corner of the high walls, and watches as she easily springs over the armoured fortifications with fox-like agility. He takes her cool hand and they start running through the heavy fields of fruit.

The air is sweet and cloying; the summer is over and the over-abundant crops are now rotting. Mashed-up fruit underfoot slows them down, and they run but go nowhere, slipping and sliding on the spot.

Meanwhile, Genesis has unleashed its hounds, and these are in pursuit, excitedly barking and slavering in the distance, their breath misting in the autumn air.

With a supreme effort, Female 198 leaps up over the pulped fruit and takes off high into the sky, lifting him with her. They sail moon-feathered into the chilly air with the Milky Way above them like a streak of spilt milk. Its irregular shape seems to map the trajectory of their flight.

Mark jerks awake, and listens guiltily to Alice's soft snoring; she is fast asleep on her back.

'You're very quiet, is something worrying you?' she asks him at breakfast.

His emotions are a toxic broth of slow-burning obsession, coupled with guilt, as he continues to brood about Female 198.

It is winter, and they are allowed one more visit to see Female 198 before she gives birth to their child. The previously bountiful green fields have disappeared, and they drive through the winter landscape, bleak and monochrome, with a watery sun sitting low on the horizon in front of them like an icy pale-yellow Cyclops-eye.

Dr Holm is his usual efficient self as he guides them once again to the Viewing Room through the shiny corridors.

Female 198

Female 198 is magnificent in pregnancy, like a ripe autumn fruit. Her gaze has softened, and her gait is slower and round as a ball. She reminds Mark of a conker: the spiky exterior concealing the rich glossy new fruit inside.

Dr Holm reassures them that the pregnancy is going well, and that the female child they have commissioned is developing excellently.

Female 198 catches Mark's eye, and once again he is aware of her knowing her own power over him. He has barely spoken to her, but she has still managed to extend her silent grasp on him.

Obsession and guilt chase each other compulsively in his consciousness like the two strands of a helical spiral. He feels sick with it, but in a strange way, he has never felt so alive …

Alice and Mark sit on their veranda, watching the three-year-old Brigit running through the June grass chasing the butterflies. The redness of her hair is starting to shine out, and her right eye is darker than her left, like her mother. She is a livewire, forever exploring, pulling things apart, tasting and testing the world with her curiosity and strong will.

She has brought a new vitality into their lives, and has filled their world with light. Mark continues to dream about Brigit's mother, Female 198, from time to time.

'Dr Holm, we are very happy with the child we obtained from you, and we were wondering if we could commission a male sibling for her, using the same parents?'

There is a silence on the other line before Dr Holm answers.

'I am sorry, but that is not possible: the mother, Female 198, has been retired. When you first met Female 198, she was 26. At 30, all our female parents are retired, that is, harvested and then euthanised, since they are past their child-bearing prime. Our policies concerning this were all explained to you in detail in your contract. We do however have plenty of other suitable females you might like to consider.'

Mark puts down his phone in shock, and looks at the little red-haired girl running round his garden, full of fire.